Praise for David Toscana'

"Hypnotic…The echoes reverberatin___
and Capistrán's distant adventures se___
tories in Latin American fiction, and ___
the tension and continuity between t___

"Toscana's underhandedly exuberant style . . . after translation, still boldly echoes the Spanish inflection.… As evidence of Toscana's exquisite control, the prose rhythm fluctuates…between the whimsical rhythms of a magical realist heritage…and a down-to-earth, everyday, contemporary realism."
—The Washington Post Book World

"Cleverly mischievous…A worthwhile and appealing sample of the new Mexican novel."
—San Diego Union-Tribune

"Toscana weaves an intricate tale that adroitly blends fact and fiction."
—Dallas Morning News

"A delightful mix of fantasy, surrealist imaginings, and folk wisdom."
—Washington Times

"[These] characters have dignity, like Carlos Fuentes's characters."
—Los Angeles Times

"A daringly intricate and haunting novel…that introduces American readers to a gifted writer who seems poised to inherit the postmodernist mantel of Carlos Fuentes.… Memorable work from an impressive new writer."
—Kirkus Reviews

"Toscana interweaves three equally compelling stories into a poignant novel of love and loss."
—Booklist

"Intriguing…a subtle and thought-provoking novel."
—Publishers Weekly

"Toscana is one of our most intelligent and subtle storytellers."
—La Jornada (Mexico)

"Toscana is the most original and enjoyable writer of his generation."
—El Observador (Uruguay)

"[Toscana's] prose is splendid, demonstrating a coherence and inventive capacity that make him unique among his peers."
—El Diario (Mexico)

TULA STATION

a novel

DAVID TOSCANA

TRANSLATED FROM THE SPANISH BY
PATRICIA J. DUNCAN

Thomas Dunne Books
St. Martin's Griffin
New York

THOMAS DUNNE BOOKS.
An imprint of St. Martin's Press.

TULA STATION. Copyright © 1995 by David Toscana. Translation copyright © 2000 by
Patricia J. Duncan. All rights reserved. Printed in the United States of America. No part
of this book may be used or reproduced in any manner whatsoever without written permission except in the case of brief quotations embodied in critical articles or reviews. For
information, address St. Martin's Press, 175 Fifth Avenue, New York, N.Y. 10010.

www.stmartins.com

Designed by Michelle McMillian

Library of Congress Cataloging-in-Publication Data

Toscana, David, 1961–
    [Estación Tula. English]
    Tula station / David Toscana ; translated from the Spanish by Patricia J. Duncan.
        p.   cm.
    ISBN 0-312-20538-4 (hc)
    ISBN 0-312-27097-6 (pbk)
    1. Duncan, Patricia J.   II. Title.
PQ7298.3.078 E7813   2000
863—dc21   99-056049
                                                                   CIP

First published in Mexico under the title *Estación Tula* by Editorial Joaquín Mortiz

First St. Martin's Griffin Edition: April 2001

10 9 8 7 6 5 4 3 2 1

To my three *viejas*:
Adriana, Valeria, and Cristina

TULA
STATION

THE DAY AFTER THE hurricane battered the city, the water level in the river gradually subsided until the remains of several cars and three buses that had crossed its path were revealed. Hundreds of bodies were found up and down the riverbed, and reports mentioned one survivor who had been swept more than thirty kilometers by the waters. The Datsun belonging to my friend Froylán Gómez turned up among the cars that were virtually destroyed. We never found his body, perhaps because he was among those thrown into a common grave without having been identified and without any attempt being made to locate family members, as the government was determined to hide as many bodies as possible to minimize the tragedy.

This story held up for many years, until Patricia, my friend's wife, came to believe otherwise.

She showed up at my house with a stack of papers (which

turned out to be a biography and a diary) and several tapes that had been recorded by an old man. She told me that she had recently begun to read her husband's manuscripts and that in them she found proof that he was still alive. Froylán, in her opinion, had taken advantage of the hurricane to fake his own death and run off with a woman apparently named Carmen. She even assured me that she knew where he was. "But I am not going to look for him," she said, "because I need him to come back on his own."

Her plan was for me to correct and organize the texts so that they could be published as a novel. In this way, Froylán would be able to read his own diary and texts as if they were someone else's, like a work of fiction that, in Patricia's words, "will make him realize that he is living a lie, and then he will want to come back to me and to the life he had before."

I do not know if Froylán is alive, and I'm not going to pass judgment on his wife's plan. I accepted the proposal not so much because of her motives but more for purely literary reasons and, especially, because in reading the manuscripts I came across Froylán's consent to do so. And given that I am mentioned several times in my friend's diary, I took the liberty of including a few notes that I felt necessary or important to clarify certain points.

With this said, I apologize for what I may have left out of Froylán's work and for what, unconsciously, I may have added to it.

—David Toscana

TULA WAS COMPLETELY silent. Not a laugh or a sneeze or a squeak of a wagon. "Vulnerant omnes, ultima necat," Father Nicanor said, and he left his church without closing the doors.

Juan Capistrán asked to be bathed early in the morning and perfumed with some lotion, perhaps to conceal the rancid odor of his flesh. They did not offer him much to choose from, and he made do with a bottle of toilet water. As he awkwardly poured it on his chest, Sister Guadalupe asked:

"Do you want me to comb your hair?"

"I can do it myself."

She opened the window, and the gentle hum of the street became a roar of cars and trucks, steps of people hurrying by, voices selling newspapers and fried pork rind. Along with the noise came a burning wind that, little by little, broke up the humidity in the room and that asphixiating sensation of being next to a chamber pot.

"Are you going to make the call for me?"

"Yes, Señor Capistrán. Right away."

The woman pushed the wheelchair over to the mirror. He picked up the comb and, with a steadiness that the other old folks envied, parted his hair on the left side, and he moved the comb through his hair over and over, as if he wanted to break open his head. In the reflection of the mirror he saw El Tuerto coming toward him, with his short, dragging steps.

"What happened, Juan? Did they already call your relative?"

"My grandson."

"Yes, him."

"Not yet. This woman is making me beg."

She looked at the two men reproachfully and left the room.

"Just tell him who I am, and that I need to see him today, that it's a matter of life or death."

But Sister Guadalupe did not stop to listen to the same instructions he had repeated so often since the night before.

With a wave of his hand he asked El Tuerto to leave him alone.

"You'll let me know?"

The *viejo* Capistrán nodded and wheeled himself over to the window. He looked out at the faces of all the women who were walking by without noticing him; he watched them from the moment they turned the corner of Madero and Reforma streets until the wall and the bars on his window reminded him of the limits of his surroundings. With each one that passed, he lost the hope of finding Carmen.

Sister Guadalupe returned and scarcely dared to enter the room. Juan Capistrán turned his head and waited a minute in silence, as he worked up the courage to ask:

"Did you talk to him?"

"Yes."

"And what did he say?"

She stood behind him. Placing her hands on his shoulders, she began to rub them gently, affectionately. She stopped after a while when she felt something similar to desire in her fingers, something that came to her not through her senses but through her memory.

"He said he didn't know any Juan Capistrán."

Fernanda slowly closed the poetry book. Her uncle had been breathing heavily for a while now and was surely asleep. She finished reciting the final lines, her voice tapering off so as to avoid an abrupt silence, changing the words if her memory failed her. She stopped the waving to scare off the flies that were hovering around her uncle's purulent leg, and she covered it with a blanket.

"What happened, Fernanda?" He opened his eyes.

"Nothing, *tío*. I was just leaving."

"So early?"

"What do you mean early, it's already growing dark."

"Then stay here tonight."

"No, they must be waiting for me at home by now."

"Okay, but don't leave without preparing a *cafecito* for me."

Reluctantly, Fernanda went to the kitchen. When she left the room, her uncle raised his head to look at her calves.

She returned after a while with the steaming cup in one hand and a small container of milk in the other. She placed them on the table next to the bed and said good-bye.

"Don't get used to these visits. They are just until your leg gets better."

Outside, the trees were filled with motionless birds, and the buzz of cicadas floated in the air. Fernanda picked up her pace, worried not about the possible dangers of the night, but rather about the scolding she would surely receive from her mother. Waking up, eating, and sleeping were governed by the clock in the entrance hall or the calls of the *horero*, the hour man; for returning home, the sun was the rule. That's why she hated the short winter days that locked her inside before five o'clock in the afternoon. In the distance she could make out the dim glow of Tula, and she thought she could even see her bedroom window.

At the intersection with the road to the Hacienda del Chapulín, she heard someone approaching. She immediately remembered her mother's warnings about the risks of walking alone. She did not want to turn around; she clenched the book in her hand in a defensive instinct. The rest happened so fast that, in later dreams, it would seem like merely a stumble.

A hand grabbed her hair, stopping her. The strong smell of mescal combined with the sensation of cold sweat running down her face. "Nothing is happening," she told herself, but a voice that spoke to her in English pulled her back to reality.

"What do you want?" she asked.

He smiled, his mouth coming closer and closer. He took the top off a bottle and emptied it onto the girl's face, back, and chest. On the verge of crying, she closed her eyes and the book fell to the ground.

When she finally arrived home, she saw the condition of her dress under the lamp in the doorway. She went inside without greeting anyone and ran upstairs.

"This is no time to be getting home."

"Maricela came looking for you three times. She said you had made plans to teach her some kind of weaving stitch."

"How rude. Not even a hello!"

"How is your uncle doing?"

"Don't think I didn't realize you were trying on one of my dresses."

Fernanda collapsed onto the bed. She needed an excuse to cry, because she would not give that man in the road even the hint of swollen eyes. She remembered the poetry book and cried uncontrollably when she realized it was lost forever in that world to which she no longer belonged, the world of beautiful verses, of her parents at the table, of her sister with longer and longer braids, of Maricela who came looking for you, of two rights and a wrong.

"*Mija*, come down right now. Your dinner is getting cold."

I AM GETTING USED to waking up at nine or ten, without rushing, looking out happily at the avenue and seeing people distressed by the minute hand on their watch, by a traffic light, by a newspaper headline.

The same thing used to happen to me when I had to wake up at six and run to the office and prepare all the answers to my bosses' questions. "Why did polyester scrap rise by three percent?" "How many tons of nylon can we get from these machines?" "Why are maintenance costs so high?" "How many workers can we lay off if we make said process more efficient?" With a little experience I found out that in business the truth is not what people want but rather answers that do not inconvenience anyone. Back then I not only wrote fiction for the literary page of the newspaper, but also for the advisory boards, memorandums, and production reports.

Patricia now looks at me sadly, as if she were looking at an unemployed man in the middle of grieving for that lost paycheck, for that world full of safety in which every day a hundred or a thousand coworkers exchange good mornings, where Japan is the anointed nation ("We have to be more like them or we're screwed"), where they talk about Juran as if they were talking about Kafka. "Have you read *Managerial Breakthrough?*" "Yes, it's a great book."

"What do you want for breakfast?" Patricia asked me.

The morning shower became a ritual. It no longer represented an act of cleansing but rather of stretching: a time to free the mind and capture the ideas that can be taken from dreams before the nature of real life blurs them.

"I don't care," I responded. The water dripped onto the floor as I looked for a towel.

"They're in the top drawer."

Ever since I'd arrived with the envelope containing my severance pay in hand, Patricia has become more affectionate and takes care of all the household chores. She says it's because she loves me; I know she is preparing herself for the end. When the money runs out, she will be able to say that she never neglected her responsibilities, she will be able to blame me for everything, and I won't have anything to blame her for.

"By the way," she shouted from the kitchen, "they called again from the old folks home."

"And what did you tell them?"

"The same thing."

And she will be able to force me to stop writing little stories and look for a real job, one with a paycheck every two weeks, a Christmas bonus, and a savings plan. "Like before," and she will say that *before* with the taste of a paradise lost.

That is why I only told her half of the story.

Don Alejo had not yet begun to snore when his wife heard the sobbing that seemed to come from Fernanda's bedroom.

"*Viejo*, don't you hear someone crying?"

There was no response from Don Alejo.

Doña Esperanza threw back the covers and stood up. With the moans, little by little, growing closer with each step, she thought about her daughter's strange behavior that evening. "She didn't even want to have dinner with us." She thought Fernanda's friends must have played a cruel joke on her, or her piano teacher had scolded her because of her clumsy fingers.

She knocked on the door gently.

"*Hija*, are you all right?"

When the only response was more sobbing, she opened the door without waiting for permission. The room was dark, and the trembling outline of the girl was barely discernible.

"It smells like alcohol," Doña Esperanza said. Then, furious, she raised her voice. "You're drunk, right? Don't lie to me!"

She rushed to light the lamp, and as she adjusted the flame to get more clarity, she slowly discovered the damaged body of her daughter, scratched and bruised, her hair messed up, and the dress with the red bow without the red bow, looking almost like a rag.

"My God!"

Doña Esperanza took a step back and lowered the flame so the room was again in semidarkness.

"Were you with a man?"

"Yes," Fernanda responded, wishing desperately that she had said no.

"Willingly?" Doña Esperanza continued her questioning, maintaining a calmness that threatened to burst.

"No." Now she wanted to answer yes.

"Just one?"

"One what?"

"One man."

"Yes, one. Is that not enough for you?"

Enraged, Fernanda wanted to get up and kick her mother and say, "What do you care? Instead of interrogating me like a criminal why don't you sit on my bed and cry with me while you stroke my hair."

"Do you know who it was?"

"Yes."

"Who?"

There was a long pause. Fernanda stopped crying. She thought of the man on the road and re-created the scene in her mind as best as she could, with one difference: the woman who was yelling and kicking was her mother. "If only it had happened to you," she mumbled.

"Who?" her mother asked again.

"The gringo who makes mescal."

"The gringo," Doña Esperanza said to herself. The gringo. The one she had once seen on the street with his shirt unbuttoned. When he had greeted her in English with barely a word, he had made her blush and lower her head. He passed by, and she enticed him with her eyes until a lady she knew scared off her fantasies. "Careful, Esperancita, that your eyes don't fall out." "Don't be ridiculous. I'm looking at him out of curiosity."

She pounced on her daughter and took her by the hair, not to stroke it but rather to pull her up onto her feet.

"Don't just lie there," Esperanza said, her calmness bursting, "stand up, stupid! Stand up and start jumping! Jump up and down until all the gringo inside you comes out!"

Fernanda did not want to jump but she did; again and again, with her eyes closed so that she couldn't see herself in the wardrobe mirror, listening to the jingling of the lamp and the creaking of the floor every time she landed. She clenched her fists and jaw and repeated to herself, "This is not happening. Today I did not go to see my uncle and I am not jumping up and down and I am not awake. It is still yesterday; yesterday morning."

"What's wrong, Doña?" Buenaventura, a forty-year-old black woman who had worked in the Gil Lamadrid house since she was a girl, appeared in the doorway.

"Help me fix up this girl, negra. Prepare one of your concoctions so you can cure her and clean her up for me. Ah, and careful not to say anything to anyone, especially Teté. She, more than anyone, must not know."

Doña Esperanza returned to her bedroom. She settled back into bed next to her husband. His eyes were open, staring up at the beams in the ceiling.

"I suppose you heard."

"Enough to imagine what happened."

- 14 -

"And what are you going to do?"

Don Alejo wanted to sleep. He was tired of solving his daughters' problems. "What fault is it of mine? Why can't they defend themselves?" He recalled the day almost forty years ago when a mob of insurgents had attacked Guanajuato and he had wanted to take advantage of the confusion and take a girl who had been snubbing him for some time. "But *she* knew how to use her nails, not like these *viejas* that from the Our Father have only learned 'Thy will be done.' "

"You should have given birth to two men."

"I asked you, what are you going to do?"

"I'll tell the gringo that I'm not buying any more mescal from him."

"That's it?"

Don Alejo did not answer. He turned over in the bed and curled up under the covers.

She lay looking at the clothes rack. A well-ironed pair of pants and a leather jacket with gold fringe hung there, the sign of order and good education for a man who had been formed in the ruggedness of the countryside. Doña Esperanza smiled ironically, thinking that this was all just a sham, and that to honor truth, it would be more fitting to see a corset hanging on the clothes rack.

"Tell Fernanda to stop jumping or she's going to bring the house down."

I WANTED TIME TO WRITE a novel; a novel for which I still have no ideas. That is why I spend my time writing these useless lines, with the hope of finding in them a possible plot or, at least, to ensure that I keep writing daily, the supposed discipline of a writer.

I wanted to run away from my coworkers who would say, "I like literature, too," and would fill my desk with acrostics, desiderata, and thoughts of love. "Look, this one is very good." And he read, "If you love something, set it free. . . ."

The opportunity came when management announced with great regret the need to downsize the company.

That same day telephones began to ring. The calls were from the Human Resources Department: "Please come by to arrange your settlement." For some, the world came tumbling down when they hung up the phone.

"I was laid off," someone said.

"You were fired," I clarified.

My phone, on the other hand, was quiet. I didn't want to wait the entire morning or leave things to luck, so I went into the office of my boss, who, in turn, was nervously looking at his telephone.

"Am I on the list?"

He stood up and patted me on the back, smiling.

"No, Froylán," he said, waiting for some sign of my gratitude.

I negotiated for hours until my resignation and severance pay were finally authorized. On my way out, I ran into a group of coworkers looking in the direction of the offices, as if the director were suddenly going to appear and tell them that it had all been a mistake and they should go back to work, that the company was incapable of stealing jobs from such loyal people who had given their services for ten, twenty, or thirty years. They were staring, their faces distorted, overwhelmed by a mixture of sadness and shame, thinking about how they were going to tell their wives and children.

I didn't wipe the smile off my face until I got home, when I feigned a look of distress.

"I was laid off," I said to Patricia.

WHEN FERNANDA WOKE UP, she did not feel any of the pain that had bothered her so much the night before. Buenaventura was by her side mumbling a monotonous song, hoping to lull her to sleep.

"Is it morning already, *negra*?"

"Yes, *mi niña*, and it's already getting dark again."

"I slept that much?"

"Last night I fixed you a *jumilla* tea."

Fernanda got out of bed and opened the curtains so she could look out over the balcony. On the left she could see the gray outline of the Cerro de la Cruz, and on the right that of the Cerro del Camposanto. Down below, the plaza was filled with people walking in high heels or huaraches, and the *horero*, hoarse and reluctant, announced that it was seven-thirty. Throughout Hidalgo Street, the cloth awnings in the marketplace stirred and you could hear the sound of horses walking across the cobblestones.

"If I shout from the balcony what happened to me, do you think they would feel sorry for me or laugh?"

"What good would either their laughter or their pity do for you? It's better for you to be quiet, lest something bad comes to your mama if everyone finds out."

The house was completely quiet. It was dinnertime, but the sound of silverware clinking against plates and the conversations recapping everyone's day were absent.

"And Teté, *negra*?"

"The señores took her to San Luis. Just until everything passes."

"But why her? The normal thing would be to send me away."

"Now you see, *niña*, that's your mama's way."

"What lie did they make up?"

"She thinks you have tuberculosis."

Fernanda smiled in an attempt to stave off her anger and repeated Buenaventura's words, *until everything passes.*

"When do they think it will all be over if it turns out that I am pregnant with that gringo's child?"

"Don't even think that, *niña*. But if that's the case, it will be God's will."

"Well, tell your god that I am not going to accept a child from that gringo, anyone but him."

"All we can do is wait."

"Look, *negra*, I prefer never to know."

Fernanda went over to the wardrobe and took out a thin housedress with a pleated skirt. She put on some flat shoes and brushed her hair without looking in the mirror.

"Go stand outside the casino and send me all of those you see who look like foreigners. I will be in the cellar."

Buenaventura was dumbfounded. She moved her eyes just enough to avoid staring. Fernanda put on the dress and went toward the door.

"Go on, *negra*, you're not going to make me go and offer myself, are you?"

Buenaventura left the room, her steps unsure and her eyes troubled. As she was going down the stairs, her lowered head turned back, hoping to hear an order to stop. She only heard Fernanda saying, "Hurry up, *negra*."

The señores returned a week later, feeling as if they had left half their lives in San Luis. Don Alejo posted a guard in front of his house because for several nights after their return, men were still coming to knock on the cellar door.

"What could those drunks want?" Doña Esperanza asked.

"I don't know," Fernanda replied.

"Me either," Buenaventura added.

"The price of gasoline went up again."

"Oh."

"The opposition insists that the elections were fixed."

Nowadays, Patricia never misses the news. She had always loved television, but she would only watch soap operas and musical shows. With the news, she had found a way to tell me that outside there was a real world, a world that we should open our eyes to because, whether we liked it or not, it's a world we can touch, eat, and buy; a world so far from the one of "your stories that might be nice but which are full of lies and things that never happened."

She also shows me newspaper clippings that her mother gives her: engineer needed with x years of experience in such and such. Salary commensurate with experience. And I, playing along, put on my suit and say, "Let's see if they hire me." I lose myself in a café all morning reading—that is, if I am not distracted by some passing legs—and I return home at midday.

"They'll let me know," I tell her. Or: "They already hired someone else."

Today was one of those days. She gave me an ad from a factory that specialized in bricks, bathtubs, washbasins, and flooring that was looking for an industrial engineer, someone with experience similar to mine.

"This job was made for you."

The factory was located in a café across from the main bus terminal, and the interview consisted of asking the waiter for the check. I went home, not hungry, with the sense of having increased the remote possibility that Patricia suspected what I was doing, and I felt ashamed for lying to her like a child.

"How did it go?"

"Fine, let's see if it's a yes this time."

As usual, she gave me the day's news, only this time it came by telephone.

"They called again from the home."

I ignored her and went into the kitchen, pretending to be hungry. I stirred the boiling soup with a spoon and heated up a couple of tortillas.

"I think you should talk to that old man," she suggested timidly.

"And what made you change your mind?"

"Because now instead of it being a matter of life or death they said it's a matter of money, a lot of money."

"All right, Patricia," I said after thinking about it awhile. "Tomorrow I'll go on over there."

Doña Esperanza came and went about the house, restless, saying to Fernanda, "How do you feel? Let's see if God will help us and not allow this." Curiosity finally got the best of her, and she began to poke around in her daughter's things to find evidence of what was worrying her so much and affecting her sleep and her appetite.

"Shouldn't it be that time of the month already?"

"Yes, Mama, almost."

But another week went by and the rags were still white, no need for Buenaventura to boil them and soak them in vinegar. Fernanda, in an attempt to prolong the deception until she could come up with a solution, gave Buenaventura a small jar so she could collect some blood from the pig that they were preparing to sacrifice for Teté's welcome-home party.

"Yes, *niña*, on Friday I can get it for you."

"But I need it today."

"If I kill it now, it will be rotten by Friday."

"Just prick it in the back."

No one noticed the pig wailing. No one saw the *negra* washing the knife.

"Look, Mama, it came."

Doña Esperanza did not have to examine the rag very closely. She slapped her daughter and threatened to throw Buenaventura out if she found any evidence of complicity, for well she knew that pig-blood stains looked different. She had learned this just before she got married, from an aunt who gave her instructions before her wedding night. "The chicken's, Esperanza, is the most similar." Fernanda felt a burning sensation spread over her entire face. Then she felt herself being pulled by the hair and then dropped, with a shove, onto the bed.

"Stop lying and tell me what you are going to do," the señora said with a renewed calmness, now that she had laid down the rules of the game.

"I don't know."

"You don't know."

Doña Esperanza began to walk in circles, laughing with mockery as she shouted over and over, "You don't know . . . you don't know." She ran her fingers along the surface of the furniture without showing any interest in the layer of dust that was sticking to her fingertips. "You don't know. . . ."

In the adjacent bedroom, Don Alejo was listening to the voices and the laughter and thought that something funny was going on. It surprised him, since in that house there were not usually many reasons to laugh.

"What's all the fuss about?" he asked as he walked toward his daughter's room.

The question was all it took for the silence to return. Both women turned their back on each other. They did not know whether they should speak angrily or sweetly, or if it would be better to just end the conversation altogether.

"What's going on?" Don Alejo smiled expectantly from the doorway.

"Nothing," Doña Esperanza replied, pointing at the girl. "It so happens that this stupid girl is pregnant and doesn't know what to do."

Fernanda could not decide whether to show her humiliation or not. She thought she would probably look less despicable if all of a sudden her eyes popped out of their sockets, if her arms came off and began to slither across the floor, or if any other terrible thing happened that would at once turn her into a victim deserving of all human pity.

"And so?" Don Alejo said, turning to his wife.

A memory flashed through Fernanda's mind: that of Lieutenant Villalón, the one who had gone to fight against the gringos and had his arm blown off in the first battle. He returned decorated and proud of his injury. "Why don't they honor me? In the end, mine is but an injury of the same war, of another defeat against the same enemy."

"I've had it worked out for days," Doña Esperanza proclaimed.

Fernanda's pregnancy was made official, and with this came the first bouts of nausea and the desire to throw up more than just her breakfast.

"It is the gringo's child," she would confess to Buenaventura later that night.

"We don't know that, *mi niña*, it could be any of the others."

"No, *negra*, I feel like I'm carrying the devil inside."

On Thursday morning Don Alejo was surprised not to hear the pig, after it had been so restless the previous days. "He's certainly aware that the end is near." He looked out into the backyard and saw it lying down, motionless, with a large infected patch covering its entire back. Doña Esperanza sent word that the welcome-home party was postponed, and she sent orders to Teté to remain in San Luis until "your sister recovers from this disease that has us all so worried."

I HAVE AN UNCLE whose image, when I try to recall it, gets confused with that of one of my elementary-school teachers. That happens to me frequently: I want to picture a face, and another one, without fail, gets in the way. Today, as I was going to see the old man, something similar happened to me: I was trying to picture an old folks home and I would inevitably picture a mental hospital, full of old people, yes, but old people who had lost their minds, with chains on their ankles and locked up in rooms with padded walls.

I parked my car in front of the stone building with the address that Patricia had given me. This big, old, rambling house showed no indication of being a home: no sign, no old people looking out the windows. I pulled the cord that was hanging from the door and heard a bell, followed by "Who is it?" It seemed like a stupid question to me.

"I'm looking for Juan Capistrán," I said, and to the eyes that appeared through the opening in the door, I added hesitantly, "I don't know if he is staying here," thinking that *staying* was not the right verb.

"Are you his grandson?"

"That's what I've come to find out."

"Come in." The door opened, revealing a kind-looking nun. Inside there was no padding on the walls or machines from the Inquisition or crazy people running back and forth. You could hear low voices, lamenting or praying perhaps, and you could see elderly men and women sitting in rocking chairs or around a checkerboard. The patio was full of plants in pots that had been improvised from empty fruit cans, and in the center stood a stone fountain whose motionless water was a breeding ground for mosquitoes.

"He's over there," the nun said, pointing down a half-lit corridor.

All the old people on the patio were looking at me by then, with a rude curiosity. I chose to ignore them and kept my eyes on the nun's back, otherwise I would have felt the need to challenge them with a "What are you looking at?"

"Are you Sister Guadalupe?"

She didn't answer. She stopped in front of an open door.

"Señor Capistrán, your grandson is here."

Two men were in the room. One of them, blind in the left eye, smiled at me without saying a word and went out into the corridor. The other one, who was sitting in a wheelchair, got upset when he saw me.

"You should have told me you were coming. How terrible!" He nervously ran his hands through his hair and straightened the collar of his shirt.

It irritated me to see him like an old maid who suddenly finds herself accosted by the man whom she has been spying on through a half-opened door. After a few seconds he calmed down a bit and stretched out his arms.

"Froylán, so long waiting for you and you surprise me like this."

"How are you, Señor Capistrán?"

"Don't talk to me like that, I'm your grandfather."

I denied this with a nod of my head. Even though they had died many years ago, I knew my grandparents well, and I was not inclined to accept stories that my father wasn't really my father or other melodramas of the kind.

"Well, I am really your great-great-grandfather," he said, "only that word scares me."

I still did not believe him.

"So how old are you?"

"Don't ask me that. Why don't you tell me how you are instead."

I was growing impatient. I could already see myself sitting at one of the tables on the patio, having a tiresome conversation with the old man as we placed the pieces on the board. "Do you want to be red or white?"

"No, Señor Capistrán, that's not why I came."

It was probably just an instant, but he looked at me for what seemed like a long time with a mixture of sadness and neediness.

"You came to talk business."

I nodded.

"Then sit down, muchacho. I am going to ask Lupita to bring us a cool drink."

Around that time a French boat had docked in the port of Tampico. And although this was not unusual, it was always news for the *Tultecos*, especially the *Tultecas*, who were waiting impatiently for the different goods that would be on board.

Authentic caravans of merchants, wagons, and convoys were organized to cross the rocky road that stretched sixty leagues and took them four, five, or six days depending on their desire, strength, and the condition of the road. Some carried gold coins and letters of credit, orders of payment and guarantor's signatures, so they could negotiate the best wholesale price for jewelry and other fine articles with the most favorable credit. Others would show up with the money saved from not having eaten or their winnings from the cockfights, with their usurious debts or a deck of cards in their pocket, so that by bargaining, swapping, chance, or mere cunning, they could get ahold of the costume jewelry and goods that the hawkers and sailors themselves were trading.

That time, Don Alejo had also gone to Tampico along with the caravan of merchants and peddlers, although with a very different purpose. When Doña Esperanza had first suggested it, he had emphatically refused because of his old habit of rejecting any plan that came from a woman.

"Go to where that boat is and buy a husband for Fernanda."

"Not a chance."

When he thought about it a second time, it seemed like a good idea. He was lured by the possibility of being in a market of white slaves where his money and his index finger could take control of lives and destinies. Afterward, he would sit back and do nothing, foisting all the responsibility onto his wife: responsibility for his daughters, for the hacienda, and for the mill. "Today I am retiring as head of this household." He felt like an old man and noticed his wife's hunger to take control. "Let her take over, so much the better for me."

"Find a nice-looking one."

"I don't know how to tell that."

"You know very well, Alejo."

Doña Esperanza crossed the street, then the plaza and another street, and went into the church to arrange the details of the wedding. "A week from this Sunday, Father." Father Nicanor was surprised by the proximity of the date and Doña Esperanza had to make up a story about a French boyfriend, a military man and skilled equestrian, who had been madly in love with her daughter ever since he'd met her on a trip to Veracruz. And now, after several dozen passionate letters, he was coming, prepared to make her his wife under the law of the Almighty.

"And you can understand, Father, that being such a busy man, he will only be here in Tula until that Sunday."

Two swallows flew across the nave and into a nest up in the beams. Father Nicanor wiped a cloth across his wide, wrinkled forehead. At that time the dog days of summer had set in, and the church had become a pot of boiling beans.

"Stop your tales, señora, and tell me if the Frenchman you are talking about is the father of the child."

Doña Esperanza did not have the courage to carry on with the lie, since the priest had already embarrassed her enough with his incredulity. She discarded responses like "What child?" "I don't know what you are talking about," and "Don't be so evil-minded," opting for:

"The Frenchman is a stranger, Father, and I will save the name of the one who got my daughter pregnant for a better occasion."

"Then you are in the wrong place, señora. The theater is two blocks down the road."

Now the swallows flew in the opposite direction and out the main door to the street. Doña Esperanza said good-bye to the priest and followed the path of the birds.

"Ah, Father." She raised her voice from the entrance. "I forgot to tell you that we will probably be moving to another city, maybe to Zacatecas. Or maybe we will go to the United States, now that they are closer. So forgive me if I don't have time to organize the benefit, and forgive my husband, too, if in the commotion of the move he forgets to send you the contribution for the new bell tower."

Father Nicanor was astonished, for he had always regarded Doña Esperanza as a pious woman. Now she left him with the bad taste of a bribe, something very different from the arrangements that he had made in his office, but not here, in the church itself, in front of the image of St. Anthony, next to the Fifth Station of the Cross, and over the crypt where so many holy men and women whose names were now forgotten rested. His hand trembling, he wiped the cloth across his forehead again to dry off a different, sticky sweat that was not a result of the heat outside. He knelt down in front of the altar and thought about the half-built tower, about the plans for the school, about his wanting to have a clock that would tell the time in Tula. "At any rate," he justified, "Fernanda will be better off with a stranger than with her mother." He called to an altar boy who was in the plaza talking with some of his friends and scolded him for not preparing the things for the next mass. He ordered him to fill the chalice with hosts and told him to bring a carpenter with him first thing in the morning to repair and varnish the pews, "then tell Señor Robles to make the stained-glass window of the Virgen del Rosario and go to the tailor and order a set of vestments."

"Yes, Father," the boy responded to each request.

"And tell them to send the bill to Doña Esperanza."

Since I had sat down to eat, Patricia had not even touched her soup. She reluctantly nibbled at a piece of bread and began to throw small pieces into her glass of iced tea. Not until I had eaten the last bite was she convinced that she would have to start the conversation.

"What did he say?"

"Who?" I didn't feel like telling her anything, but playing dumb was not the way to avoid the interrogation.

"The man at the home."

"Oh, him. He wants me to write his biography."

"His biography? So who is he?"

"He says he's my great-great-grandfather."

"I'm not talking about that. I mean he must be a famous person, a politician, a businessman, an artist. People don't ask you to write their life story if they don't have anything interesting to say."

"I don't know about before," I said, "but now he is just an old man in a wheelchair."

She thought for a moment before hurling the next question at me.

"Is he going to pay you well?" Her eyes revealed the hope of having a husband with a salary again, like those of her friends.

"We didn't talk about that." I didn't want to tell her that, judging by appearances, Señor Capistrán probably did not have a penny to his name.

"But you are going to talk about it."

"Maybe," I replied, annoyed, before retiring to the study.

Patricia's interest in money irritates me, even though I myself know that the only thing that would take me away from my novel and writing that biography would be money. Money to write.

Sᴜɴᴅᴀʏ ᴡᴀs ᴀᴘᴘʀᴏᴀᴄʜɪɴɢ and still no news from Don Alejo or the fiancé. Doña Esperanza, with her eyes fixed on the road to Tampico, was calming herself down, saying over and over, "He's going to get here in time," only then to immediately undermine her attempt to convince herself with, "And if he doesn't get here?" Whom would she have to get back at for Father Nicanor's laughter, her daughter's swollen belly, the hypocritical reaction of Tula?

On Friday night, Buenaventura heard a few knocks on the back door. It was Don Alejo, disheveled and foul smelling, his mottled beard half-grown. He was accompanied by a young man whom he told to go inside immediately so that no one would see him.

"How was the journey, señor?"

"Fine, *negra*." Don Alejo took off his boots with a sigh of contentment. He stretched and wiggled his toes for a few seconds.

"Have you eaten, or shall I fix you something?"

"First let the señora know that I've brought her son-in-law."

Doña Esperanza had seen them coming down Morelos Street, and although she was calm, happy almost, her joy was for the arrival of the fiancé only. On the other hand, Don Alejo's arriving in time made her furious, for she was left with no reason to tell him off.

"The señor says—" Buenaventura began, but the señora interrupted her.

"Tell them to take a bath and we'll sit down to dinner shortly."

Doña Esperanza notified her daughter that the men had arrived and showed her what dress to put on: "The green one. The full one with the high neckline."

But when the two women came downstairs, Don Alejo and the sailor had already begun to eat with a hunger that allowed no room for etiquette. The only greeting was a brief "How was it, Papa?" which received no response. Doña Esperanza observed the appearance and manners of the newly arrived with intense displeasure. Long, thin hair with no sign of ever having been combed; a prominent nose that deviated from the axis of symmetry. At least he was big and tall, but he made noise when he chewed and held the fork as if it were a farm tool.

"I told you nice-looking," Doña Esperanza mumbled, annoyed.

"I chose him from a bunch of sailors, not Bourbon princes. Anyway, he has the advantage of speaking Spanish well."

Fernanda did not take her eyes off him, fascinated by the man's exotic looks. She felt a mixture of tenderness and fire. Tenderness because of his timid look, almost childlike, and because of the pleasure he took in gobbling up his dinner; fire because she was comparing him to the boys from the casino, those from that night; because for several weeks she had forgotten about the piano, weaving, poetry—weeks thinking about bodies and sweat. She observed his thick, callused hands, and his lips, how they moved while he chewed the little that he did not swallow whole. She turned toward Don Alejo and said softly, "Thank you, Papa." She considered herself fortunate to have run into that gringo on the road to Tula. Otherwise, she thought, Teté would now be in that chair.

"What's your name?" Doña Esperanza asked with no other interest than to break the silence.

"Giovanni," he replied, stopping a moment to take another bite, "Giovanni Capistrano."

"So where are you from?"

"I'm from Naples."

"Good-for-nothing," she addressed her husband. "I told everyone that he was French."

The man kept eating, completely indifferent, as if no one had told him that in less than forty-eight hours he would be married to the girl across from him.

Today I went to the home again. I arrived prepared with notebook, pen, and a Sony tape recorder that had cost over one hundred thousand pesos, which until now I had considered wasted. I found the *viejo* Capistrán in his wheelchair next to the window, and I assumed that he had been watching me since I had parked the car. I decided from now on I would park on the side street.

"How have you been?"

"Fine, Froylán."

He showed no sign of joy; he didn't even ask the obligatory "And you?" That made me furious. I was expecting those open arms again, his nervousness to see me, his hands rising to the collar of his shirt—in short, that same behavior that had irritated me the first time. Nevertheless, I had been the one to clarify my role as a businessman, and it was absurd to think that he would again offer me the role of recently found grandson.

"Well, here I am," I said stupidly.

We sat for a while in silence. I ran my fingers through my hair over and over as if I needed to know that it was still there. He scratched his forehead, neck, and ears with his index finger. It was a tense moment in which I could not find the appropriate words, so I chose to be direct.

"In order to begin working, I need to know how much my fee will be."

The *viejo* Capistrán wheeled his chair over to the bed. He leaned over and lifted up a small chest from which he removed a crumpled, yellowed envelope.

"Here," he said, sticking out his hand, "see if this is enough."

I put my index finger and thumb into the envelope, thinking that I was going to pull out a wad of bills. In that brief instant I thought of denominations of fifty thousand; I calculated, added, made plans; I became greedy. My fingers removed a sheet of stamps. Out of sheer inertia I counted them: there were seventy-eight, all the same, colored in blue: 50 centavos Correos México. In the center was the profile of a man staring left who, although he looked nothing like the priest Hidalgo, I knew immediately it was him, badly drawn. I assumed that the complete sheet must have been of one hundred stamps and at some point the other twenty-two had been torn off.

"And this?" I again asked stupidly.

"Some stamps," he said with a mocking smile. "They must be worth something. Why don't you take them to a philatelist so he can tell you how much?"

I felt I had returned to the most primitive level of business: my work in exchange for stamps. I could already see myself bartering every chapter of the biography for a sack of cocoa or a fox skin.

"And not a word about the stamps to anyone around here, because I've been living in this place thanks to, I don't know, taxes or donations, and if they find out I have some means of payment, they will look for a way to collect even for the toilet paper."

I felt a chill run through me when I thought that instead of selling the stamps I might start collecting them. But I knew immediately that I was safe from such idle passions. And so I had nothing to lose by visiting the Association of Philatelists to ascertain the amount of my salary. I told him I would be back later, not knowing for sure if I would return.

"Leave me your tape recorder so that I can start telling my story."

"Do you know how to use it?" I inquired, thinking about the possibility of risking the more than one hundred thousand pesos and because I sensed that it was just a trick to ensure my return.

"Of course." He raised his voice, staring straight into my eyes. "I am old but not a fool."

DURING THE WAR WITH the United States, the Mexican government offered land to the foreign soldiers who would give up their weapons. It was said in Tula that my father had been one of those deserters. Almost nothing was known about him: he owned a few acres near the Hacienda del Chapulín, he became fond of mescal, so much so that he began to make it for his own consumption and, after mastering the trade, distilled it in quantities sufficient to sell throughout the southern part of the state. As for the rest, there were many contradictions: some said that he never returned to Tula, others were sure they saw him once or twice in the market. They said he was handsome, some women remarked, and they all wanted to see him, to meet him. He did not speak Spanish. Yes, he did. He was tall. Not so tall. Not even the farmhands who worked with him agreed on their description of him. They spoke of their *patrón* as if they were speaking about a vague memory, about an image clouded in fog. My family did associate with him, because my grandfather would buy him the mescal that he would later resell to the cantinas. The only thing for certain is that nobody knew his name and that, although a secret to many, I was his son.

"When we get to your country, will you teach me Italian?"

"Yes."

From her table, Fernanda looked with disdain at her guests, her friends from school. The man next to her made her feel superior to them, to those women destined to make do with a *Tulteco* like poor little Miguel or the good-for-nothing Alfredo, and she thought of even harsher adjectives for the other *Tultecos*.

"Will you take me one Sunday to see Pius IX?"

"Yes."

Now it all came down to getting on a boat, clinging to Giovanni. She was overtaken by the same arrogance that until then she had so detested in her mother, and she noticed that she was beginning to become like her.

"Make sure I see Florence."

"Yes."

Even Doña Esperanza was satisfied. With his hair cut, beard shaved, and custom-made suit, he looked worthy of Fernanda. What's more, being a natural show-off, he behaved like that fictitious military man and skilled equestrian she had met in Veracruz.

"And, of course, Venice."

"That, too."

Fernanda was growing tired of her white dress, the congratulations from so many unknown women, of the girls who were going up to Giovanni to ask him anything just to be noticed, to be wanted, just as all the sailors on that foul-smelling boat will want me, accustomed as they are to being with prostitutes with hairy armpits, and seeing me on the arm of one of their colleagues, they will be struck with envy.

"Let's go now."

"Not yet."

At the urging of Doña Esperanza, a chorus was organized that called repeatedly for Fernanda to go to the piano. She did not want to leave her man, but she decided to accept. This way she would be able to impress him with an Italian piece and show him as well that she was not just a body.

"I'll be right back."

"All right."

In the short distance to the piano, several señoras approached her to hug her, pat her on the back, and to talk to her. "Congratulations, *hija*," said one. "May God give you many children," said another, and a devout woman whispered to her, "Even though he may be your husband, he can't force you to do things you don't like." And Fernanda smiled so as not to insult them.

She sat down at the piano and turned toward her husband in search of his approval, like someone waiting for the wave of the baton. Gently, her fingers began to press the keys, and everyone was quiet, listening to the piece. Fernanda was concentrating so as not to make a mistake because from that point on it would be "our music." She finished just as many of the guests were starting to get bored. The applause was halfhearted. Fernanda thanked them as she looked for her husband among all the people, looking toward where she had heard the loudest applause.

"And Giovanni?" she asked her mother after not finding him.

"Come, *hija*, let's go to your room."

They went upstairs like ghosts.

Doña Esperanza closed the door and asked Fernanda to sit down on the bed. Anxious, she obeyed, looking at the two large chests where she had placed all of her things she would need for the trip.

"*Hija*," the señora said, clearing her throat, "you must understand that Señor Capistrano already kept his part of the agreement."

Downstairs, through all the noise, the guests thought they heard a cry, but they just as well thought they heard nothing at all.

I RETURNED TO THE HOME shortly after noon. A red light on
the dashboard of my car indicated that the engine was dangerously
hot. It was no surprise: a month ago summer had turned on its
heat. If I rolled the window up, I would suffocate; if I rolled it
down, it was like opening an oven to see if the cake was done.

Fortunately, with its dampness and thick stone walls, the home
was a refuge of cool air.

"I was talking to your tape recorder," the old man said, excited
to see me come in.

He clutched it between his hands in a way that reminded me
of the devotion with which my grandmother would hold her rosary. I pictured my tape recorder moist with the old man's sweat,
but I didn't say anything.

"Did you go to the philatelists?" he asked.

"I just came from there."

"And what did they tell you?"

I looked inside the envelope to make sure the stamps were still there.

At the association I had been served by a fifty-year-old man, one of those who, in wanting to be so kind, seems like a bureaucrat looking for a promotion and makes you anxious to leave. "Of course, with pleasure, right this way, sit down, would you like something to drink? Do you smoke? Are you comfortable? My friend, what heat, aren't you one of the Gómez del Cercado family? You really don't want anything to drink? At your service, it's no bother whatsoever." That excessive friendliness made me sense an ulterior motive, and it filled me with suspicion.

"Okay," I said, not so much because I was thirsty but more so that he would be quiet, "I'll have a glass of water."

With the belief that there was something improper in offering water, he replied, "No, my friend, you will think that we don't want to attend to you properly," just like that, in the plural, as if more people were there, and he opened a bottle of grape drink.

"I didn't think they sold these anymore," I said so as not to have to thank him.

"Well, the truck keeps supplying us."

I took a few sips to be polite while I explained the purpose for my visit. I took out the sheet of stamps and placed it on the desk. He picked up a magnifying glass and began to look at the stamps.

The man, whose name I saw no need to memorize, placed the magnifying glass on top of some papers and opened a book that contained hundreds of drawings of stamps in black and white. In alphabetical order he looked for the M for Mexico, then slowly scoured the pages, mumbling softly, "Hidalgo . . . 1872 . . . blue." His finger stopped on a line and then moved over to a calculator.

"Do you want to know how much your stamps are worth?"

His expression alone was enough for me to realize that they

were worth a lot, but I did not trust the man, nor would I have trusted the figure from his calculator.

"No," I said.

My throat had become dry, and I drank the grape drink without hesitation.

The *viejo* Capistrán stirred restlessly in his chair and, impatient with my silence, repeated the question:

"What did they tell you, Froylán?"

The longer I put off responding, the more his hands would sweat on my tape recorder.

"That as of today I am your biographer."

AROUND THE TIME I was born, things began to look good for Tula. Commercial routes changed as the border came closer, and we benefited the most. In addition to what had always disembarked in Soto la Marina, Matamoros, and Tampico, hundreds of convoys with goods from the United States began to pass through Tula. Mules that had traveled from Virginia with tobacco that would be smoked in Chapultepec went down the street I lived on, as did the Stokely & Sons wagon with a pair of recently turned and varnished wooden legs for former president Santa Anna, which had to be redispatched to his retirement hacienda. And if the gringos sent us a large amount of merchandise, we would send them lots of mules loaded with coffee, istle, and henequen. Business weakens the memory, and soon we forgot that we had recently been shooting at them. Tula began to grow not only because istle producers like my grandmother were making a fortune, but also because every convoy left behind a trail of money from customs duties, sales taxes, and rights of passage. Inns were soon set up for the muleteers and their teams, and warehouses were built for the cargo. The condition of the roads was improved and they became primary routes, and Señor Zurubarán included Tula on his stagecoach line. Although the government paid a team of men just to clean up the manure the animals left behind on the streets, the stench became constant and the complaints of certain important señoras forced the construction of a road that would go around the city. Merchants arrived and built big houses along the river, and they laid down a sidewalk that was soon used for the obligatory Sunday stroll. On one side of the Cerro de la Cruz, the construction of a small fort was initiated and stopped several times because of the differing opinions and proposals of the eight presidents we had had in the five years since I was born. Finally only a pile of stones and four standing columns remained, something like a church that had collapsed, because once President Comonfort said that there was no money for luxuries like that, everyone else agreed. Tula would have to defend itself. All the *Tultecos* armed themselves with at least a rifle, and my grandmother—this is the last time I will call her that—proposed hiring a retired general to organize a small army to safeguard us from the enemies. A month later an advertisement appeared in the country's major newspapers: position available for a retired general to take charge of the defense of Tula, Tamaulipas, good pay. And in parenthesis: Much higher than the government pension. In small print was the information of whom to write to and a note telling candidates not to send details with respect to their military careers, only their names, and a selection committee would be responsible for doing further research.

As I usually do when I am coming from the eastern side of the city, I took the street that passes by the cemetery on my way home. Many years ago the long walls were white; now they are covered with all kinds of names, mostly foreign or illegible, sayings that destroy the reputation of some girl, threats between gangs, and ads for Coca-Cola or the candidate of the moment. Today a message signed by a so-called Pinez caught my attention. It was written in excellent calligraphy in fresh red paint, as I'm sure it was not there yesterday. *A lifetime is a short time to wait for you.* I did not care what the sentence meant, but it struck me as sublime among such stupidity.

Don Alejo went to look for Dr. Isunza after Buenaventura said, "My God, this is too much for me."

He knocked on the door for a long time, careful so the noise would wake only the inhabitants of that house and not the neighbors. With the thought of Fernanda suffering, he started knocking louder and louder until his knocks became downright aggressive.

"Give it up, scoundrel, I'm not going to open the door!" a woman yelled.

"Open up, señora," Don Alejo insisted, "it's an emergency!"

The bolt slid open and a woman appeared.

"I'm sorry, I thought you were my husband."

"So he's not here?"

"He came home drunk a little while ago and I threw him out. When he's drunk, he's unbearable and . . ."

Don Alejo left her talking to herself. He wasn't in the mood for marital conflicts with a daughter crying in pain and in the hands of a servant who was saying, "This is too much for me." He blamed himself for having waited until the last minute, for not having looked for Dr. Isunza after the first pains. He might have found him at home, or in the casino or in the cantina, with barely one drink in him. Or he could have looked for him weeks ago, when it was obvious that Fernanda's belly had grown far beyond what was normal; or from the day Buenaventura had said, "That child is upside down," and not money or herb drinks or the efforts of a masseuse who labored for hours would turn him around; or from that Sunday when in the middle of mass Fernanda had started to shout, "I'm carrying the devil inside me," and since neither the priest making the sign of the cross or the words of the other people had quieted her, she had had to be lifted up by six men and taken home.

He scoured the town looking for a drunk and staggering shadow. He walked through the streets inspecting every corner, in part because he felt it his duty to exhaust all possibilities, and in part because he was a coward, afraid to return home and hear the cries of childbirth. As he was passing the casino, he spotted a shape on the stairs and went over to it.

"Idiot," he said, and with a kick, he made Dr. Isunza roll down into the street.

He stood him up and with weak shoves made him walk. Isunza did not protest; he allowed himself to be herded, like a sheep.

On the way home, Don Alejo wondered why he was dragging that man to Fernanda, and he thought of taking a detour, going to the river and throwing him in the water to calm himself down and to give himself a good excuse for his powerlessness. But he did not want to go home empty-handed. He carried the doctor to the door and forced him upstairs.

A few steps from his daughter's bedroom he heard the uneven crying of a newborn, the suppressed crying of Doña Esperanza, and the hysterical crying of a shattered Buenaventura.

COUNTLESS LETTERS BEGAN to arrive, since in peacetime retired generals were a species that multiplied by the hundreds. Although it had been requested that they be brief, most sent long lists of names, dates, places, and victories. One had fought alongside Morelos, another swaggering about having saved Iturbide's life on a certain occasion, and another proud for having participated in his execution. I am still very young, wrote one, but I fought in Chapultepec and if I had been killed, I would be a national hero. I am among those who remember the Alamo. I was imprisoned in San Juan de Ulúa for eight years and they never forced me to confess anything. It wasn't that the committee considered this information insignificant, but the extra pages added ounces and increased the postage. To avoid the task of checking the backgrounds of all of them, the committee decided to consider only the names they knew. And so, they read off the name of the sender from each envelope, and the panel would say that one yes, that one no. Father Nicanor attended the meetings and requested more than once to be allowed to take part in the selection. I have to be sure, he said, that you are not going to bring some priest-eating liberal here. But the committee refused again and again. Here those who pay decide. Of course if you would like to contribute…And he explained that it was not for lack of money or desire, but that it was impossible to allot church money for military purposes. If you don't cooperate, prepare to live with the consequences. The father told them that he had been so insistent because he would have preferred that they willingly allow him to take part in the matter. He tolled the bells that morning and, followed by the crowd that had gathered, ran through the streets carrying a banner of the Virgen del Rosario. When they passed by the houses of Doña Esperanza, Isunza, Maradiaga or Madariaga—I've never known how it is pronounced—and those of other wealthy families, the crowd shouted long live religion, long live our Holy Mother Rosario, long live Isabella II. That afternoon Father Nicanor went to the selection committee again and Dr. Isunza, furious, reproached him. Don't you realize that they can execute you for what you did? The father explained to them: today you heard only "long live," tomorrow we may shout "death to." With all in agreement, the priest was accepted into the committee and they returned to their work of sorting through the names until only four were left. Dr. Isunza suggested organizing a public event where the entire town would be informed of the name of the general chosen, and it was agreed to hold it on Saturday, which would allow time to come to an agreement as to which of the four was the most competent. On Thursday, however, weeks after not having received any more applications, a letter arrived from Peru. Throw it out without even reading it, the lawyer, Maradiaga, said. But Doña Esperanza said no, that she had a good feeling about it and it was best to see who had sent it. The discussion began as to whether to open the letter. That we are receiving it now is reason enough. It's like in novels: whatever happens when no one expects it, turns out to be the most important part. Why wait for them to agree, Doña Esperanza must have thought, and she opened it. It was one of the few letters that had respected the small print in the ad. It said only Xavier Pisco and gave a home address in Cajamarca. I think we have found our man. Please, señora, we have no idea who he is. What's more, how many months will it take to get him here? Yes, señores, but just think that our four candidates have left a trail of enemies across the country. On the other hand, General Pisco will arrive here with no past; nobody knows him, he is not responsible for any deaths, he's never betrayed anyone, and he is free of any scandal with women; nor are creditors after him, nor does he owe any pawnshops. Everything you say makes sense, señora, but if we buy without seeing, we could well get some huarache-wearing illiterate who has only fought with stones. And who loves the sun more than anything else, the father added. Look, Doña Esperanza said calmly, twenty-two years ago I made the mistake of picking the wrong man, and I never make the same mistake twice.

I OPENED UP MY NOTEBOOK and on the first page I wrote: *Juan Capistrán, first interview*. Then I was quiet for a while, not knowing where to begin. My only experience as an interviewer was with a couple of engineers who were looking for work, and now, for lack of ideas, I began interviewing the old man as if he, too, were unemployed.

"What's your full name?" I asked the first of my absurd questions. I continued with generalities such as where he was from, date of birth, and marital status.

The *viejo* Capistrán smiled without responding, and he looked at me with the compassionate eyes of a teacher about to reproach a bratty student. I kept on going with new questions, looking for the right one.

"Froylán," he finally said, "what I want is to tell you a story."

I ripped out the page and he began to talk about a woman

named Fernanda, an uncle, and a gringo. About a place called Tula.

"Tula, Hidalgo?" I interrupted.

"No," he said, bothered, "it's in Tamaulipas."

"Sorry, I'm not very good at geography."

"What you are not very good at is history."

He continued to tell his story. I made a point not to interrupt again; if in the end I still had any doubts, I could use my imagination to clear them up, to tie up the loose ends. Only now it wasn't me who interrupted.

Steps could be heard in the corridor, and they stopped outside the door. An old woman, with a face of someone who smells something rotten, looked at me for a few seconds, until she could no longer contain her laughter. She revealed her toothless mouth and left shouting, "Come see Juan Capistrán's grandson."

I waited a few seconds for the result of that cry, the response of the other old people. Nobody spoke. Nobody came. Then I noticed that the *viejo* Capistrán was still talking as if nothing had happened, as if his memory were spilling over with no way to stop it.

"Wait." I felt my hand asleep, about to drop the pen. "Give me back the tape recorder."

"I am paying you to write," he said harshly. Then, when he saw my irritation, he softened. "Lend it to me, Froylán, I need it to talk to when you're not here."

I could not find a good reason to refuse, and the only answer I could come up with seemed childish: "Okay, but just give it back to me when you're done." I chose not to say anything.

THERE WERE FOUR CEMETERIES in Tula. One had initially
been located on the outskirts of town, next to what had been the
temple of Rosario, but then, as the village grew, it ended up being
almost in the center of town. It was the oldest one, authorized,
in fact, by Friar Juan Bautista de Mollinedo, founder of Tula. Ordinary people were buried in this cemetery, those who had not
stood out for either their good works or their faults; people who
went to mass on Sundays and to confession every so often. Another cemetery was three leagues away. Those who had led dissi-
pated lives were taken there, as if they were contagious lepers,
because it was said that evil spreads from soul to soul. Another
one was the small crypt beneath the altar in the church; this was
authorized only for those who the father called *cuasi sanctus*. And
finally, one more cemetery was on the Cerro del Camposanto,
where those who had died with their faith in doubt were buried.

On the hill, they said, one was closer to heaven and farther from hell. So, he who was between rising and falling was given a push upward. That is why it was not permitted to dig graves that were more than a yard and a half deep. The decision of who was to be buried where belonged to Father Nicanor, who found the pleas of a widow to be extremely annoying whenever he chose to send a man to the cemetery three leagues away.

After administering the holy oil to Fernanda he pointed in the direction of Cerro del Camposanto.

"But my family has always been buried in the crypt," Doña Esperanza argued.

"It would be better for you not to object," the priest said, unwilling to compromise, "because for you I have in mind a place farther away."

On the way there, the only crying was from the newborn baby. The father talked and talked and prayed until they had covered the casket with dirt. Buenaventura took the baby's arm and made him wave good-bye. On the way down the hill, two white-haired men were quietly discussing the injustice of dying so young.

"What a waste," said one.

"That's the luck of the draw," lamented the other.

Just then the sun was beginning to disappear, and from the kiosk, as he saw them coming, the *horero* shouted, "Seven o'clock and Fernanda rests."

The Gil Lamadrids went home and bolted the door shut. They needed time to deal with their anger and frustration.

"We are going to have to tell Teté," Doña Esperanza said.

"She may already know. This kind of news travels fast."

"And Buenaventura?"

"She went with the baby to church for a while."

"If she returns," the woman said, her voice breaking, "don't let her in."

Doña Esperanza would forever blame the baby for Fernanda's death. Don Alejo, on the other hand, would blame himself, without holding Dr. Isunza at all responsible. This is why he began to drink, and during one of his many drunken binges, and perhaps while asleep, he fell off his horse, which had wandered far away. He was found several days later, almost a skeleton, on top of an anthill, and it was never determined if he died because of the fall or because of the bites from the red ants.

WITH ALL THE ECONOMIC progress and the competition that had begun between the cities in the state to see which would prosper the most, the people of Tula became very proud. We have always preferred to call ourselves *Tultecos*, because we considered the natural name of *Tuleños* to be undignified. Another reason for our great local pride is due to the maestro Everardo Fuentes. That story begins around 1840, a time when the first pianos arrived in Tula. Soon after, a few music schools and academies were founded, and as time passed, deep rivalries were formed between the maestros as well as the students. But music was merely an activity to occupy the leisure time of the well-to-do, and the schools taught it as entertainment. The excitement came when I was three years old. After having spent more than a decade in Vienna, Maestro Fuentes returned to our country. He was offered many opportunities in the capital, but he said that his mission was in Tula and that he would convert his native land into the musical center of the world. That's what he said, and

I think he achieved it, at least for the piano manufacturers. Before you knew it, we were overrun with upright pianos, grand pianos, baby grands, diagonals, black ones, white ones, black-and-white ones, German ones, Dutch ones, and French ones. There was such a great interest in music that at get-togethers Bach and Beethoven were discussed just as Puskas and Distéfano are today; excuse the bad example, I think I am a little behind the times when it comes to soccer. Maestro Fuentes condemned the old schools and took on the task of creating real concert pianists. He exacted discipline, schedules, rehearsals, performances, and he came up with the idea of organizing what he called the Concert for One Hundred Pianos. He gathered together all the pianists, and beyond what he expected, 207 showed up. Most of them were able to fit in the plaza, and those that did not fit had to be accommodated on side streets, leaving some still in the wagons in which they had driven there. After suggesting a melody that all would know, the maestro, from the kiosk, conducted the hundreds of volunteers and the five violinists whom he had hired for the event. What had been planned as the greatest musical event of the century turned out to be the greatest chaos of notes in history. All because they hadn't rehearsed, accused some and justified others. Maestro Fuentes explained by saying that the synchronicity with his baton was perfect, but because the area in which the pianos were distributed was so large, the synchronization of sound was impossible. Who knows, but he never tried a concert like that again. The local press downplayed the failure and said that the important thing had been to show the imposing force of music. As a result of such rationalization, in Tula the concert was considered a huge success. However, Maestro Fuentes's main contribution to the pride of the *Tultecos* was not that event, nor was it for making the piano fashionable, nor for the good reputation of his school, nor because he considered himself a personal friend of Liszt; nor was it because he had a diploma with high honors from the Austrian government signed by a Hapsburg, which hung on the front wall in his study in a frame with gold borders and a glass that protected it from yellowing.

I STILL KNOW VERY LITTLE about Juan Capistrán, and although his story had barely gotten to the point where his mother dies, I thought I had enough material to start writing.

I decided to begin with what could have happened when the gringo raped Fernanda. I locked myself in the study and in two hours I had a version of the events, from the point when the girl stops reading poems to her uncle until she returns home, with the exception of the exact moment of the rape. I spent another two hours immersed in scribbling and target practice with the waste-basket.

My imagination dried up in that white gap in the middle of the chapter.

I have fantasized many times when making love to Patricia: I rape her savagely. I turn her into a robust fighter who tortures me to unspeakable limits. I picture even the smallest details: I hear her cries or mine, I see the blood, the marks from the blows and from the ropes. However, I know that the bed is one thing and the desk is another.

I need inspiration, I thought.

I assumed that my wife, always so fond of the ordinary, would find it perverted if, while we were making love, I were to pick up a pencil and start writing down in a notebook everything I was thinking. I found a more reasonable solution in the entertainment section of the paper.

Just my luck, the Lírico was showing *Endless Rape*.

I hurried over there, since the last showing was beginning in fifteen minutes.

I watched the worn-out film in which a woman was the victim of countless humiliations, with all the erotic energy that such humiliations aroused, and how her attitude suddenly changed and she came to ask for what before had been imposed on her. After eating a couple of hot dogs with lots of *picante*, I returned home with no ideas but with the desire to endlessly rape my wife.

"Patricia," I said to her several times without waking her.

It was useless, and I had to go to sleep, thinking only about the *horero* in Juan Capistrán's town.

"Twelve o'clock and Patricia rests."

Buenaventura kept trying for almost two years. First every day; then her attempts were more spaced out, letting months go by between them. She would knock on Doña Esperanza's door: "Señora, I've brought you your grandson, take pity on him." The answer was always something like "Go away, *negra*, that baby killed my daughter." Buenaventura would turn to go, promising to return again, a promise she would make habitually, in accordance with the dictates of her conscience; a promise that one fine day she did not want to keep. "And if Doña Esperanza accepts the baby?" She realized that she wanted him for her own, as she had not even wanted her beloved Esperancita, her deceased daughter.

She had named her Esperancita in honor of her *patrona*, but Doña Esperanza, far from feeling honored, reproached her audacity. Conflicts over the name did not last long: a loose pig killed the newborn, and so as not to be left without any signs of motherhood, Buenaventura kept her breasts in production, squeezing them while she prepared coffee or while nursing starving orphans. Thanks to that she was able to breast-feed Fernanda's baby, and in this way she realized that, as he grew, he was more of her blood, and she didn't care that he was covered with pimples and that instead of hair an almost white fluff had sprouted, because the less he looked like the Gil Lamadrids, the more he would come to be her child.

Others, however, did not look favorably on this.

"Did you see how ugly Esperanza's grandson has become?" one señora said quietly.

"Yes, Chole, it has to be because he's taking milk from the *negra*."

"You don't really believe that," another commented.

"Oh, yes. I know for a fact that Buenaventura has been breast-feeding him."

"Yes, but I was told that the *negra* produced wild boar's milk."

Since Fernanda had shouted "I am carrying the devil inside me," many things had been said. In Tula, those words were taken as a premonition, and they gave rise to many evil stories even before she died giving birth.

So, if the baby got sick, they spoke of God's punishment, and when he got better, it was a pact with the devil. It was said that when he was just a few months old, he had begun to make obscene gestures and had erections. Someone spoke of having seen scales on his back, and if later they had the chance to see him with no shirt on, his skin ordinary with no defects, instead of discrediting the rumor they would say, "The *negra* removed them with sandpaper."

Father Nicanor, worried about the boy's soul, checked his files at church. "He's not even a Christian."

He proposed baptizing him as soon as possible, and naively, he went to see Doña Esperanza.

"That boy is going to turn into a devil if he's not educated in a good home."

"The boy has a father. Look for him."

"You must understand the seriousness of this. He's not even two years old and they say that he is already after the girls."

"You don't believe that now, Father, do you?"

The priest blushed and went back to his church. He spent the night there praying. The following morning he ran to the goldsmith and asked him to engrave the back of a medal of the Sacred Heart. He paid a few reales, which hurt, but he felt even worse for giving up the old medal.

"Here, Buenaventura, and be sure he always wears it around his neck."

She thanked him for what she thought was a friendly gesture, and while they were discussing the date, time, and godfather for the baptism, she offered him a coffee. Father Nicanor thought about a wild boar running through the church. "No, thank you," he said. After they said good-bye, she looked admiringly at the small medal and, with difficulty, read the engraving. *Lord, this is your child, too.*

BY ORDER OF THE former president Santa Anna, the Ministry of Public Works, Colonization, Industry, and Commerce published the notice for the writing and composing of the Mexican national anthem. The maestro Fuentes knew immediately that it was his chance to make history. Tula would be the birthplace of the nation's anthem, which would be sung throughout the centuries, in every school and for every event and for every war. Until then he had been less successful than he had hoped in creating musicians who would themselves be famous and applauded. Now he would work for his own glory. When he found out about the procedure for the competition, he became indignant down to the core. First, a poetry contest was called for, and then, once the winner was announced, a competition to put music to those verses would be held. How can that be? Maestro Fuentes asked himself, and he started to pound on the keyboard of his piano. Music came before the word; by right of antiquity it has the privilege of governing the other lesser arts, because compared to music, they are no more than handicrafts. The greatest of Quevedo's poems is not worth much more than a clay pot, but the most modest of concerts by the least worthy of composers is more valuable than our lives. And so he went around complaining for weeks; he even sent a letter of protest to the high official in the ministry, so he could voice his indignation. Subsequently, when the winning poem had been selected, a limit of two months was given to put music to it. Infuriated, Maestro Fuentes began to compose, and only because the insistence of a few señoras convinced him: come on, show the world you are a genius. But he refused to read the poem. Just count at the verses and tell me where the syllables are accented. He worked day and night, without their having to lock me up like that would-be poet, he said, and fifteen days prior to the deadline he traveled personally to the capital with his score under his arm. Then it was time for waiting, nail-biting, insomnia, and bad moods. Four months passed without the panel's reaching a decision while Maestro Fuentes grew old at an alarming rate. Those good-for-nothings, he thought, letting off steam over a drink, they give half the time to compose that they take to decide. The day the official paper came out with the announcement, there was a kind of mourning. Everyone spoke quietly, no one played a piano, and stores and pharmacies closed, opening only for emergencies. But in Tula, the blow lasted only a day, and a short while later the pride that I was talking about was revived and strengthened. We did not accept the music of the Spanish composer who had won, as we found out that Maestro Fuentes's defeat was due to the panel's ill will toward him for his letter of protest, and he having turned in his score personally, his name did not even appear on the list of competitors. The following September 16, on the celebration of Independence Day, the national anthem was sung for the first time, to the music of our maestro. And so it would be forever.

From the moment I got out of the car I could hear the effeminate voice of a troubadour determined to imitate Silvio Rodríguez. The bar was faintly illuminated by candelabra that hung on the walls, and wherever you turned, there were photographs of Pancho Villa.

"Here I am," said David Toscana as I walked over to his table. .I had called him that afternoon using a mysterious tone that I later regretted. "I have a matter involving money," I had said and invited him to the bar. He did not even ask what it was about.

I sat down at the table and opened my portfolio on one of the vacant chairs.

"I want to ask you two favors."

Before ordering anything or even deciding if I wanted a drink, a large man wearing a bandanna brought me a tequila.

David spoke to me about his novel, and I told him of my intention to write one and about my economic situation, which would become unsustainable if I didn't make some good money.

"Sell your car," he told me. "If you want to be a writer, live like a writer."

"First I want to sell this." I handed him the envelope with the stamps.

He looked at them for a couple of minutes, between sips of his lemonade.

Sometimes I lie out of necessity or convenience; now I did so out of mere impulse:

"I inherited them from an aunt."

"How much are they worth?"

"*That's* the first favor I want to ask you."

He let a moment go by while he waited for me to continue. Finally he said, "Do you think that I . . . ?"

"Yes."

"No, Froylán, when I was a child, I collected some stamps from the 1970 Olympics, but you need an expert who, to begin with, can tell you if they are fake or not."

He put the stamps back in the envelope and handed them to me.

"Although now that I think about it," he said as he took the envelope again, "I know someone."

He stopped there. He put the stamps in a folder, stood up quickly, and left a five-thousand-peso bill on the table.

"See you later," he said.

I sat there wondering if those five thousand were enough to cover his check or if he was already cashing in in advance for the favor. Through the open door I could see my car, and I pondered the possibility of selling it. Before closing my portfolio, I saw the pages I had written about the old man. David had left without my having asked him for the second favor: I needed his help to edit them.*

*This is the consent to which I referred in my introductory note. (D. T.)

Doña Esperanza learned that her grandchild was finally going to be baptized and sent a note to Father Nicanor demanding that he give the child the same name as Fernanda's husband. But since the priest felt that the name Giovanni Capistrano was too much for such an unfortunate creature, he decided to name him Juan Capistrán, not knowing if Capistrán was a last name or a middle name.

Not even during the ceremony could the father block out of his mind the stories that had gone around town.

"He is making fun of God," he exclaimed, because when he poured holy water on him, the boy smiled.

"Father," Buenaventura explained, "he isn't a baby anymore, don't expect him to start screaming."

The baptism had been postponed several times because no one would take on the role of godfather. "Lest I set Providence against me," responded one of the candidates. After a dozen refusals, Buenaventura went to Abelardo Morfín, a strolling player who often visited the town and who, because of his occupation, found in the stories about the boy not a reason to fear but a reason to laugh.

There was no baptismal gown or money from the godfather, no fiesta, no tamales. Just the minimum amount of words necessary to carry out the sacrament and the vows of strictness.

"Give this to the boy," Abelardo said as he left the church, handing Buenaventura a package.

She struggled to untie the strings and ended up tearing the paper. Surprised, she discovered a bronze dagger and accepted it with the obligatory fuss.

"But this must be worth a lot."

Once he had a name, the people could no longer talk about him as they had. Now he was Juan Capistrán; Juanito as they began to say, and the name gave him importance, humanity, and he no longer represented that abstract character with the devil inside and scales on his back. Almost everyone forgot the stories, and Juanito began to grow more in stature than in wisdom.

YEARS LATER, A crack had opened up in the ground collapsing two of the three walls that composed the fort project, and when nobody was expecting him, General Xavier Pisco arrived, tired and in a sorry state. He would later explain his tardiness by saying that when he wanted to enter the country through Acapulco, he was deported; when he tried the journey by land, he got mixed up in the civil war of some Central American country and fell prisoner; and when he landed in Veracruz, malaria had wiped out all his strength and put him one step from the grave. With his gentle foreign accent, he asked for the mayor. He is in that yellow building, the *horero* told him, and once inside the building he asked again. The person in front of him answered: That's me, what can I do for you? He put aside the weary posture of a traveler and stood at attention with military stiffness. General Xavier Pisco, and he added proudly, head of the military force of Tula. Ah, yes, the mayor responded, astonished, please be so kind as to sit down, and he ran to the casino, to the church, and to Doña Esperanza's house to say, I have the Peruvian in my office, what the devil do I do with him? It had been a long time since any Lipan or Comanche had come down from the hills, a long time without holdup men on the nearby roads or gunshots from the capital to determine who would be president now, two years since the fort had finally fallen, the fort that, they said, in the end we didn't need. Well, tell him thank you very much for bothering, but that another time it will have to be, and send him back to Paraguay. Peru, idiot. To Peru, then. And for hours they talked about it with no one accepting the blame for having brought him, much less the responsibility of supporting him. News of this man who had come from so far away piqued the curiosity of the town's people so much that a group went to look at him in the office with the curiosity and sickness of one who goes over to look at a dead person, and as he was sleeping, resting from his long journey, he looked just like a dead person. Father Nicanor anxiously joined them, prepared to ask this man a thousand questions, but when he saw Pisco had a crucifix hanging from his neck, all of his doubts were removed. This man stays because he stays.

PATRICIA WOKE UP, AND the first thing she did was to give me a kiss. She got up to wash and I watched her legs until she disappeared behind the door. Those legs that I liked so much to grab and that led me to get married.

Things change a lot depending on the mood you are in when you wake up. "I'm coming," I yelled, and now in the shower I wanted to tell her the truth about my job, tell her I love her, tear up the pages about the old man, return the stamps, go back to that calm and monotonous but happy life, to that time when I thought just as she did and novels were just a slow substitute for television.

It was the fiesta of San Antonio, the patron saint of Tula.
The procession passed through the streets with songs of forgiveness and lively dances. Peasants came up from the plains to pray
to the saint, and families came from neighboring towns to hear
music and visit the fair. As they passed in front of the statue of
Friar Juan de Mollinedo, women threw roses, and the dancers on
foot and on horseback would circle it two or three times. Father
Nicanor led the group and, with his arms in the shape of a cross,
began each song, and the others joined in. "Look, *alma mía*, at
Jesus hanging on the cross . . . ," until they all ended up in the
church, still singing and ready to hear mass.

Nothing remained of that party atmosphere when the priest
began to celebrate the mass.

"Wake up, Juanito, how disrespectful," Buenaventura whispered
as she nudged him with her elbow.

He was trying to concentrate on what the priest was saying and was moving his legs to stay awake, but the church was more crowded than ever and the air was stagnant.

"I'm going over to the door to get some air."

"Go on, muchacho, but no going outside."

The warning was of no use, and Juanito went out to the plaza. There he walked through the stands of fried fish, candles, picture cards, games of chance, and shooting games, mindful of the progress of the mass so he could go back right at the end. He spent a few reales to play dice and enjoy his bad luck because, after all, no one knew he was there. "Dominus vobiscum," the powerful voice of the priest could be heard all the way out there. Juanito filled his mouth with candies and chilacayote, and he asked the price of everything that was out of reach. "Fiat voluntas tua." He looked at the bamboo structure that would soon be shooting off colored lights and smelling like gunpowder. "Dei gloriam." Just to be sure, he decided to take another look at the church, and in the middle of the street, not knowing if by accident or fate, a girl came into view, "the way they say virgins appear on the road to perform miracles," he would later say.

"What's your name?"

"Carmen, and yours?"

"Juan Capistrán."

"Your name sounds familiar."

"If we had met, I would remember."

"Aren't you the one who has the tongue of an iguana?"

Juan opened his mouth to show his tongue.

"I don't know," he said without pausing to reason, "I don't know anything about iguanas."

Carmen waved good-bye and went off into the distance. He could not follow her, something was holding him to the ground.

"When will we see each other again?"

"Never," she said, and turned the corner on Guerrero Street.

He lost sight of her. Then he began to notice the odor of waste and manure from the many horses tied to the trees and benches and iron fittings in the plaza. He did not hear the murmur coming from the church nor did he know that mass had ended until he felt the blow.

"I told you not to go out."

Juan staggered for a few seconds and then collapsed without ever putting his hands down.

"What's wrong, *mi niño*, I didn't hit you that hard."

The *negra* knocked him about without getting an answer. She asked for help and two men offered to take him home. He was carried, bewildered, and with his eyes wide open but not looking at anything in particular. Once in bed the remedies came raining down: sal ammoniacs, crushed artemisia, boiled fennel with cinnamon. "This never fails," Buenaventura said, and she began to prepare the balsam of González. She bought soapwort alcohol, plasters of Andrew of the Cross, cress dipped in milk, and she went back to the pharmacy for more sarsaparilla powder. She tried fomentations of hellebore water, rattlesnake ointment, and Catholic oil that was taken to the priest. "I don't give my blessing to these things," he said, refusing at first. "Come on, Father, it's for a miracle." "If the people find out, they will ask me to bless cough syrup." More valerian infusions, cataplasms of Guillermo Servidor—nothing would bring him back. One, two, three days without sleeping, without his expression changing. "A medicine," Dr. Isunza recommended; "a prayer," suggested the priest; "another herb," Buenaventura decided.

Abelardo arrived in Tula to work during the fair and he had barely entered the town when he was informed that his godson was not well. "They say that now the devil has gotten inside him for leaving church, even though they also say that the *negra* left him an idiot with a blow to the head." Abelardo stood in front of the sick boy's bed and, after looking at him for a moment, began to laugh.

"Let me have him for a while, *negra*, and I assure you I will bring him back cured."

Buenaventura helped him throw the boy over the back of the horse and said good-bye to them with a blessing.

Abelardo returned with the boy around midnight. The two were falling-down drunk, but they came on their own feet. Juan looked bothered and pointed his finger at Buenaventura as if she were responsible for something. He handed her an almost empty bottle of Gringo Amigo and kept on going all the way to his bed.

"I am not going to forgive you for this, Abelardo."

"Look, *negra*, Juanito is too young to have the problems of an adult. But it happened, and that's that, there's nothing we can do about it. Now he will have to recover like a man."

Since the liberals had been in power, the father feared that they would expropriate his church and turn it into a gambling house or, even worse, give it to an Anabaptist who would conduct his work of proselytizing after burning the crosses, painting over the paintings, and whitewashing the facade to convert the modest baroque style into simple, plain walls. When they questioned him about supporting the Peruvian, he said that some savings could always be taken from the alms. Doña Esperanza found out about this and raised an outcry. Even though we don't like it, she commented to the important men, we should pay the general's salary or the church will have warlike powers on top of that which it already has. It was agreed that he be paid 120 pesos per month and that every wealthy family pay a share to cover the cost. After improvising a roof for the ruined fort, Pisco dedicated himself to evaluating the risks of an attack on Tula and the possibilities of mounting an effective defense. He scoured the outskirts, indicating on a map the suitable points for carrying out ambushes, open-field battles, and positionings for artillery. He plotted the best and worst routes for the advance and retreat of the troops. He asked for entrance to all homes to analyze the thickness and material of the walls, and he determined which ones could best serve as a refuge and which ones had the best rooftops on which to place snipers. He went up the surrounding hills and, drawing parabolas, envisioned different scenarios in which the city would find itself under attack. He placed markers on streets to indicate where trenches should be dug and parapets set up. Finally, going door to door, he took an inventory of the weapons at his disposal, including some kitchen utensils, sword-shaped letter openers, and even my bronze dagger. After a month's work, he informed city hall that Tula's index of defensibility was 207 on the Aaronson scale, and since nobody was familiar with such a scale, he had to explain in a few words that the city would be easy prey for any gang with more than ten rifles and average levels of courage. Then he called for a volunteer military service. Better yet, make it mandatory, Maradiaga said. No, señor, Pisco refuted, those who are obligated to serve are the first to defect to the other side. Most of those who were of age enlisted in the service in order to receive the basic training, and only Maestro Fuentes lamented that two or three of his most promising pupils had given up their enthusiasm for the piano in exchange for the sword. Intense debates were held to determine if there was more honor in music than in weapons. What would become of our religion, Maestro Fuentes questioned, without all the music that makes us feel it? And what would have come of our independence, Dr. Isunza refuted, if instead of slaughtering Spaniards we had played them a farewell tune? In three months the *Tultecos* learned the language of the bugle, how to light the fuse of the old cannon on the Cerro de la Cruz, and more importantly, how to identify the escape routes.

In the end it was not hard for me to sell the car. The image of a fat wad of bills alleviated any sense of attachment. What was hard was buying the Datsun. I went to the market with a fixed amount so as not to be tempted to spend more. I walked among the cars asking prices and haggling over figures without finding anything that fit my budget, until I came across an authentic piece of junk. That's the one, I thought, and after some brief negotiations I drove my Datsun in the direction of the home, with a good amount still in my wallet.

"Look at it," I said to the *viejo* Capistrán when I got to the home. "Have you ever seen anything so horrible?"

He wheeled his chair over to the window and stared at it for a while.

"Will you take me for a ride? It's been a long time since—"

"Another day," I interrupted him dryly. I was not excited by the obvious difficulties of getting that man in the car.

Ever since I was a little boy, whenever I acted selfishly my conscience would nag at me insistently. Nevertheless, I was certain that this sense of guilt would die in a few minutes, much less time than what it would take for me to give the old man a ride.

"Yes," he answered after the fact, "of course I have seen more horrible things."

His face changed completely; it became distressed, stiff, his eyes searching for something far away in both time and distance. Afterward, I told myself that I should not have asked, but curiosity got the best of me.

"Like what?"

"Froylán, have you ever been in love?"

"Answer the question I just asked you."

"I am answering it."

"Of course, with my wife."

"That's not true."

I was about to tell him to go to hell.

"Are you sure?" he said before I could talk.

"Of course I'm sure."

"Then you aren't lying, you are simply mistaken."

Deciding to leave, I went over to the door. My relationship with Patricia was confusing enough without someone stirring things up even more.

"Froylán, you have to find Carmen," he said desperately.

Awkwardly, I said good-bye and hurried to leave the home and reach my car. As I was trying to stick the key in the lock, I turned around. Grasping the bars like a prisoner, the old man was looking at me, his eyes wide open and filled with tears.

"Look for Carmen."

As if it were part of a long treatment, Juan took what Abelardo had given him as medicine. He began to feel the need to have a drink every time he thought of Carmen. At first he did it secretly, as he had agreed with the *cantinero* from the Lontananza, who, collecting a surcharge for the risk of being accused of corrupting a minor, gave him a bottle of mescal per week. As time went by, his fondness for alcohol became known, and he was able to drink in front of everyone, buying his bottle from whoever would give him the most for his money.

Buenaventura broke down in tears each time she heard her boy singing drunken songs about a haughty woman who would soon pay her debts of love. But she never wanted to interfere for fear that he would fall back into bed, rigid and dumb, and with perhaps no hope of returning to the world.

"Take the bottle away from him," she finally said to the priest, "so that if he dies or becomes crippled, I won't be to blame."

"And don't you think that dead people weigh on my conscience, too?"

Not all the effects of the alcohol were negative, and that eased the sadness of the *negra*. Hair began to grow on Juan's head, and the pimples that covered his face slowly became faint scars. Dr. Isunza did not know how to explain the healing effects of the mescal, which is why Father Nicanor attributed it to a small miracle.

"Be very careful," Isunza warned him, "don't give the entire town justification for getting drunk by saying they're drinking something holy."

"And where will I find her? In some cemetery?"

"No."

"It's already a miracle that you are alive; don't expect another one."

"It's not a miracle, it's Carmen's fault."

I had returned to the home sooner than I had planned. I had wanted to at least write the chapters in which Juan turns to drinking, because the old man is using the tape recorder to move through the story at a rate I cannot keep up with. I had thought about visiting him just once a week, on Wednesdays, and writing the rest of the days, but the crushing recollection of his voice asking me to look for Carmen, his hands grasping the iron bars on the window with the urge to break them open, was enough to make me go back.

"Why do you blame Carmen?"

"Are you willing to help me?"

"Why blame her?"

"Are you?"

I did not feel like helping him, and even the way he evaded my questions bothered me, and so if only to upset him, the answer to his question would be "No, I'm not willing." However, Carmen intrigued me, and I responded, "Yes."

He sighed with a smile.

"Then all you have to do is go outside and look carefully at all the women. You will find her in one of them."

"If that's what it's all about, then I can introduce you to an aunt named Carmen."

"Don't be ridiculous; the name is the least of it, and the face and the body are also irrelevant. The important thing is that it be her and that you know how to recognize her in some woman, in anyone that you see walking, having a cup of coffee, reading the paper, going up in the elevator—"

"Then who is she?" I interrupted before he could list every possible human action.

"How should I know, she could be anyone. I have seen her pass by this window three times, and all three times in a different woman. But I understand that I can't do anything anymore. What can an old paralytic do? The first time I let her go by, the second time I yelled and she took no notice, the third time I hurried out to pursue her in my chair. 'Crazy old man,' she yelled at me, and I lost her just as she crossed the street."

"Assuming that I believe you, how am I going to find her? I've been in this city my whole life and I've never seen her."

"Did you already write about the part of my life when I met her? Write the rest. Think about her, think about her a lot. Observe her at the fair or playing the piano or looking out from the porch at the herd of cows on her hacienda, think about her as a young girl and think about her as a woman. You will see that she has many faces, many forms, and that in the end, she is only one. Write about her again and again, a thousand and one times. Soon you will know who she is and you will know how to find her."

I felt like a character in a children's story where the prince has to find his loved one in a crowd, by her shoe size, a mole on her shoulder, or by the voice with which she accompanies the songs of the woods. The only thing missing was the *viejo* Capistrán telling me that I had to find her before midnight.

"And what do I do when I find her?"

"You will know that what you have with your wife—Patricia, right?—is nothing."

"Then don't count on me." Something began to trouble me. I turned toward the door certain that the toothless old lady would be there. But no. I felt something close to fear, and as I searched for a good reason to turn down the old man's plan, I gave the first excuse that came into my head. "Remember that I am married by the two laws, church and state."

"Froylán, Froylán, it surprises me how ordinary you are, and even more so considering that you want to be a writer." After a moment of silence in which I couldn't think of any fitting word to say, he added, "Although looking at it carefully, that is just what might save you. So are you willing not to have any other woman than your own?"

I did not respond.

"Are you?"

"I already gave that answer to the priest."

"To Father Nicanor?"

"Don't confuse things," I answered, questioning the morality of hitting an elder.

The man in front of me was definitely very different from the imploring aged man of the last visit. His movements and gestures had such force that it would not have surprised me if all of a sudden he were to stand up and throw away his wheelchair for good.

"Then you can live more intensely, more painfully, than any artist or martyr. Fall in love with Carmen, desire her with all your flesh, but deny yourself from having her. Force yourself to live forever with Patricia, forever pretending so as not to break your vow. You will be the master of the most terrifying passion, of your endless decline. And then, having become a man drained by his own denial, you will see what you can write."

The offer was tempting.

Looking at it carefully, it was not an offer, it was a challenge.

But I don't have the spirit to be a martyr.

Yes or no?

What do I have to lose?

García Cubas published a statistical report of the country that created great anxiety in Tula. I don't remember the exact figures because I am bad with numbers, but it turned out that we were the second most populous city in the state, with just slightly fewer inhabitants than the capital. The señores who were bored with running their haciendas and who had turned toward politics as a way of filling their idle time said that we only needed a few more births to become the capital. We were the capital once. Yes, but that was because Governor Vital came to Tula to hide from the gringos; now we are talking about forever, of building a governor's palace and putting up the president when he comes. Then I would become governor, the mayor said. And those of us sitting at this table would make the decisions about taxes, laws, prisoners, schools, water usage, and how the state's money would be spent. How many more do we need? One hundred? Three hundred? And nobody can die. That is Dr. Isunza's responsibility. I, one of them said, am going right home, and in nine months

I will provide another *Tulteco*. All applauded and drank to expanding their families. Well, I couldn't even if I wanted to, señores, because my wife is already in menopause. Then marry off your daughters. And the men left the casino and headed home, ready to eliminate the cold showers, half acts, and the not-todays. Excitement spread to all the homes. Soon a phrase was coined: in nine months the capital will be born, or something like that. Rewards were offered to the women who brought children into the world, and Father Nicanor was shocked because he saw those gifts as an opportunity for easily tempted ladies. Some thought Isunza to be a miracle worker because he found the remedy to cure some sick people whom he himself had given up on. Others, though, did not believe they were miracles; rather they speculated on the number of patients he had let die before without making that second effort for them. The haciendas needed more workers; an announcement was made offering tax exemptions and lots of land for families that would settle in Tula, and nobody ever stopped to ask to himself if supremacy of inhabitants guaranteed political leadership. Some weddings were moved up and others *had* to be moved up. Each birth was a public event. Regardless of the time of day, as soon as it was established that the baby had not been born dead, the *horero* was sent out to go through the streets shouting the news. At such a time Mrs. So-and-So gave birth. Then came the procession to the window of the newborn to sing a Te Deum. After the announcement a few honest families with money came, but along with them came many homeless looking for a place where they could live off others. And so the Immigration Council, whose objective would be to investigate the background of those wanting to settle in Tula, was established. And to observe all the possible angles of the candidates, the council was divided into four branches. The Crimes and Offenses branch, headed by the lawyer Maradiaga, handled digging around in the state archives to determine whether the applicants had had any legal trouble. A dozen applicants were rejected when it was discovered they had arrests for vagrancy, insulting authority, urinating in public, and other minor infractions. One who had been arrested for insulting authority was arrested again, as when he was told of his rejection, he cursed the lawyer's mother. Those who came out clean from this branch passed to the Treasury branch, where Doña Esperanza subtly meddled in the wallets, assets, accounts, debts, and deficiencies of the newly arrived. If we had money, the father of one family fired back, we wouldn't be after those lots. Then came the Health branch. Dr. Isunza would look for symptoms of present diseases and signs of past ones. If found to be contagious, the sick person was escorted at a distance to the outskirts of town, having received no treatment and only a few small bottles of medicine as a courtesy. Finally there was the Morals branch. Father Nicanor made sure that the foreigners were Catholic by making them say the rosary and confess, then giving them Communion and making them say that Christ had no brothers and that the brothers referred to in the Bible were really his cousins. Listen, Father, Doña Esperanza protested, the Constitution allows freedom of worship. Look, señora, it would be better not to say anything because viewed like that, the entire Immigration Council is unconstitutional. A chalkboard was set up in the middle of the plaza where the number of inhabitants was tallied each time someone was born or a family settled. The months passed, and the excitement dwindled due to the simple effect of time and because García Cubas did not publish a new report. Then the *horero* would come out at dawn to inform all that Mrs. So-and-So had given birth, and they would yell at him to be quiet and let them sleep. The second honeymoons were over, and the women went back to their plasters and migraines and the señores kept a close watch again over their daughters. It rained, and the chalkboard was erased, without the number having been added to or subtracted from in weeks.

Sitting down, with a blank sheet of paper in front of him, Father Nicanor searched his mind looking for new arguments, a new focus for the parable of the prodigal son. If he didn't come up with an idea soon, he would have to deliver his sermon in the same words as every other year. He thought about what he would have done if he had had a son who squandered money in that way, and while thinking about it so much, he began to believe that the elder son in the parable had good reason to complain. Frightened, he slapped the paper and ran toward the altar to ask forgiveness for his human and sinful logic.

"Homini domini . . ." he had barely begun when he heard someone spit.

Father Nicanor turned around and saw Juan, with a bottle in his hand and a smile lost between his teeth. The priest stood up, prepared to kick him out. How can you even think of coming into the Lord's house to get drunk and, on top of that, spit in it, he thought with his raised hand closing in a fist. However, before getting to him, he changed his attitude to a less violent one, since he understood that spitting on the floor, even though it was God's floor, was a small fault compared to doubting the Scriptures.

"What's wrong, son?"

"I came to celebrate the feast of Santa Carmen." Juan raised the bottle as if to make a toast.

The priest launched into a small sermon on eternal punishment for those who forget their Christian life in exchange for alcohol, but he soon noticed that Juan would not feel the pain of eternal punishment but rather that of the moment, and he had to change his speech to a more worldly one.

"If you want her to be yours, you should take interest in what interests her. I don't think a poor drunk like you is going to attract her attention."

Juan looked at his face, trying to decide if that advice was honest or merely a trick to get him to stop drinking.

"Here, Father, it's yours." Juan handed him the bottle.

"No, son, mescal is not even good for drowning cockroaches."

"This is cognac."

"Well, I have a little place to keep that over there."

Juan knew perfectly well what interested Carmen, what impassioned her. Since he had seen her in the plaza, he had been wondering how it was possible that he had not seen her before, and with a bit of research he learned why: Carmen lived on the Hacienda del Chapulín, and she came to Tula only once a week, almost secretly, and spent the afternoon in Maestro Fuentes's academy.

He left the church, and the priest was not in the mood to tell him to clean up his spit. "Anyway, tomorrow it will be as dry as that drunk boy." And he felt calm because in the half-light he had seen the reflection of the small medallion, *Lord, this is your child, too.*

Juan headed directly toward the academy. For Maestro Fuentes, shaking Juan's hand was enough to know that he was not facing his best prospect.

"Your fingers are fat and short," he said to Juan.

Even so, he accepted him, since he would pay the same as the other pupils, and if he did not succeed in learning, the blame could be attributed to his hands, without discrediting the academy. As a special requirement he made Juan sign a letter freeing the academy from any responsibility in the event he never mastered the piano, "and I recognize that, the maestros being of such high caliber, I can only attribute my failure to the deficiencies of my hands."

Juan began to work in the mornings tanning leather, and in the afternoon he would go to the academy, stinking of acid, prepared to let his fingers travel over the labyrinths of the harmonic scale. He became anxious because several weeks went by and he could still not complete the basic exercises, while the other pupils moved their fingers over the keyboard with the ease of a *marimbero*. Juan's fingers kept pressing the adjacent keys at the same time, and not even stretched to the maximum could he reach the C and the A at the same time. Sometimes in the music rooms, in the corridors, at the entrance, or at the exit, he would run into Carmen, with her gray eyes and intense black hair like that of a blue raven, but he would not intend to speak to her, or even say hello, until he could play a piece flawlessly. For months he put himself through a ritual in which he would hang from a bar for a long time and then stick his hands in almost boiling water with ginger. But his fingers did not get any longer or any thinner. Buenaventura watched him sadly, not knowing if the addiction of the piano was more harmful than that of the alcohol.

But on a day like so many others, something happened.

After his usual practice, Juan went to the room where Carmen was playing, and he heard something that was not music.

"The Maradiaga's son is handsome and he plays the piano very well," a girl was telling Carmen.

"Yes, but music is for women. Men who play the piano are too ladylike; men belong with rifles."

Juan left without hiding his embarrassment. He went directly to the church and there spit, once again, in front of Father Nicanor.

"THE TELEPHONE IS RINGING," Patricia shouted from the bathroom before the first ring had even ended, as if her announcement were necessary to hear it.

"So let it ring," I responded. I was leafing through a Time-Life book on reptiles, trying to determine if it is true that rattlesnakes live in caves, and I did not want to be interrupted.

"It might be important," she insisted.

All my life I've been answering calls that *might* be important.

"Hello?" I picked up the phone to silence my wife.

"This is Sister Guadalupe."

Only photographs of a chameleon shooting its tongue out at an insect with pins stuck in it and a sequence of a snake devouring some rodent that seems unperturbed despite seeing half its body inside.

"Yes," I said after a brief hello.

"I am very sorry, Señor Gómez, but here at the home we only take care of the elderly who have no family, so you can either take him home or pay the monthly fee."

Of course what the sister felt least of all was sorry. I explained to her that there was no proof of my relationship to Señor Capistrán but that I was certain, on the other hand, that my checking account was at zero.

"Who was it?" Patricia asked as soon as I hung up.

A chapter dedicated to dinosaurs and then more photographs of crocodiles, Gila monsters, turtles, boas, and cobras, but nothing about caves with snakes.

"Nothing important again."

"I'M AT YOUR SERVICE."

Xavier Pisco looked at him for a while, smiling, scrutinizing every detail as if it were a selection process.

"Good, I've been looking for a kid like you to help us with some routine jobs."

"Like what?"

"Shine boots, for example, or run errands."

"I came to be a soldier," Juan said on the verge of punching him.

"So you want to be a boy hero?"

"No, they're all dead already."

"Yes, they should have stayed with their mamas, like you. So do me a favor and don't come back until you are old enough."

Juan left the fort and went down the Cerro de la Cruz by the northern path. He was thinking about Doña Esperanza, Carmen, and Pisco, about all those people who made up reasons to reject him: he was a murderer, he had scales, he was too young. He was thinking about the life that would end as soon as he got to the bottom of the hill and about the one that would begin at that same moment. He thought about his name: Juan like any other Juan, illegitimate son living with a *negra*, grandson of the owner of so much land that he would never set foot on unless as a laborer. The name. He decided to begin with the name because he knew that those four syllables carried a lot of weight. He went to the school library and looked for a book that he had consulted the year before when he researched something about Hernán Cortés. He found it, shiny and within reach: *Great Men of the World*. He would pick names at random. The first one seemed like a waste: Cervantes y Saavedra, Miguel de. Only one name on the two pages. The second was no better: another writer, a philosopher, and a musician, all Germans, and although Juan's skin was more browned by the sun than by his race, those names seemed to be for the soft, pale skin of a plucked turkey. He opened the book a third time. The first name in the upper left-hand corner struck him like an avalanche: Teotocopoulus, Doménico. Spanish painter born in Crete . . . He could discard the last name. He didn't even know how to pronounce it. Just Doménico was enough. Doménico sounded like a conquerer of faraway lands, adventurer of all the seas, raper of women, beheader of his enemies, protector of his followers, threat to the civilized world, return to barbarity. Doménico Capistrán? No, just Doménico. He put the book back on the shelf, and as he left the library, he felt the weight of a sword on his hip.

"Doesn't it seem stupid to have named yourself Doménico?"

"Yes," he answered with a hint of embarrassment, "but at the time it seemed somewhat grand to me, and it was enough to inspire me to go out in search of adventure."

"When did you decide to go back to your real name?"

"I haven't gotten to that point yet. Before leaving Tula as Doménico, I wrote a note to Carmen."

"What did it say?"

The old man pushed his chair over to the chest from which he had taken the stamps. He rummaged through some papers and removed a yellowed one that was folded in half twice.

"Here," he said to me. "I still have the rough copy."

Doménico

Learn this name that is not of a man but rather of a heart that sets out in search of arms and war so that you will notice him. Doménico has no other music than the thunder of guns and the wails of the injured. Doménico has no other law than that of the strongest. Be prepared Carmen, because the day you least expect it Doménico will come to steal your heart.

Tula, Tamaulipas, February 13, 1863

"And did it also cure your iguana tongue?"

"What?" the old man asked unenthusiastically.

"The mescal."

"Why would you bring that up now?"

"Just a question I still have," I responded, unable to hide my smile.

"Stop kidding around. I told you the truth. Look," he flattened his hair with his fingers, "it grew in such a way that I still have it."

"Yes, I see that, but what you can't prove to me is that as a boy you were bald."

With a jerky movement he wheeled his chair over in my direction. I thought he was not going to stop until he crashed into me, but he stopped a few centimeters away as if only wanting to show that he still had the strength to challenge me.

"Nor can I prove that my face was covered with pimples."

"No."

"Or that my mother was Fernanda or that Buenaventura raised me."

I waited for a while before saying, "Or that you are my great-great-grandfather."

Now he moved his chair backward. He went over to the window, finding his only escape; running away with his eyes from that universe of two sidewalks, one street, of men and women he hated because they walked as if they had somewhere to go.

"Keep the stamps if you want," he finally said, "but don't come back here again."

PROGRESO WAS LOCATED straight down Hidalgo Street, just before a spot with a grove of huisache trees where, because of their density and pleasant shade, the laborers rested there at midday. From there you went south to ford the river that, except in the rainy season, had such a weak current that from a short distance the flowing water sounded like someone urinating. Once across the river, a small altar was set up right where Don Alejo had died. The anthill was no longer there, since who knows when, but a Spanish naturalist, recognizing the species, had christened it the Formica Alejonea. The altar served as a boundary; nobody ventured beyond that point either on foot or on horseback because from there the Cave of the Rattlesnakes was visible.

Juan felt the urgent need to prove to Carmen just how much of a man he was, as the humiliation of the piano was still pulsing in his fingers, and having spit in church seemed like childish mischief to him.

"I am going to spend the night in the Cave of the Rattlesnakes," he told Isunza's wife, and he asked her not to call him the name she always had, now that his name was Doménico. The señora informed all of Tula about the cave, but she forgot to mention his new name.

Juan only hoped that the news would also reach the Hacienda del Chapulín.

Even though common sense was telling the boy, You're crazy, what do you gain with such stupidity? If you die there, you will stay there because no one will get you out, nobody said a word that might discourage him. Juan was offering the *Tultecos* something exciting, morbid, and everyone accepted the offer; everyone except Buenaventura, who was crying in front of Saint Lorenzo surrounded by garlic and candles.

They followed him through Hidalgo and the huisache trees across the ford and the path to the altar, and from there they saw him slowly move off into the distance, pale and trembling, they said, to the mouth of the cave. It looked dark out, and the reddish sky was becoming blacker and blacker. Juan turned around and was disappointed to see that, among all the people, Carmen was not there. He went into the cave, and everyone became silent in an attempt to hear the rattlesnakes or some cry or at least a moan.

It grew completely dark and the curious onlookers left, commissioning three men to keep watch all night from a safe distance, fearful of the cave and even of Don Alejo's ants.

Dawn came and the three men decided to return. While they were having coffee and bread at the Mesón de Mollinedo, they said that they had heard nothing, neither cries nor moans, only rattlesnakes and the current of the river flowing like urine.

I spent three days in virtual seclusion, visualizing Carmen and talking to Patricia only when necessary at dinnertime— "Why did you buy Hérdez sauce?"—and insisting that she go visit her mama: "It's been a long time since you've seen her." Even when I was alone in my study, it bothered me to hear her cough and to imagine her in front of the soap operas and the news with a big bag of potato chips, choosing the news item of the day: "The president said that now inflation really is going to subside" or "A boat with refugees sank and about a thousand people died." Her knocks on the door annoyed me—"What time are you going out?"—as did the way she wrapped herself up in bed to mean that the day is really over and another begins tomorrow.

But it was worth it; now I have a rough idea of what Carmen

is like. I have created her in fifteen pages.* The way she walks, breathes, puts on that pale, pink lipstick that goes so well with her smile whether she is having fun or not. I am still missing much of her face and body, but I think that if I see her, I would be able to recognize her.

Carmen.

Patricia did not go visit her mother; however, as soon as I emerged from my seclusion, she threatened to leave me once and for all. "You are very strange," she said, "you've changed a lot since you've been going to see that old man."

"But I love you more than ever," I said without looking in her eyes.

---

*Those pages never appeared. Perhaps he took them with him the day of the hurricane. (D. T.)

AFTER ADOPTING THE METRIC system, the government sent a stack of official papers to Tula detailing the new regulations for commercial transactions as well as a series of explanatory pamphlets. All of a sudden, because of a presidential whim, they wanted to change our pounds, cuartillos, and arrobas, our leagues, varas, quarts, and our gallons, for a set of measures that nobody understood. If you were talking about varas, everyone could picture more or less the same length, but when talking about meters, nobody could agree. How long is a meter? The question flew about. The pamphlet tried to explain it like this: it equals the ten-millionth part of a quadrant of a terrestrial meridian. The question was worth more than that answer. The señoras knew if a pound of sugar for one real was a good price, but they had no idea if the merchant was taking advantage by selling a kilo for two reales. The one who understood the numbers best was Madariaga. He was commissioned to coordinate the proper installation of the new system, and the *Tultecos* went to him at first to clarify things and later to ask him to get rid of the meters and liters. For the most part, the citizens asked out of laziness, so as not to change an age-old custom, so as not to have to adapt to new measurements, so as not to lose their ability to be amazed, since if someone told them I traveled one hundred kilometers in a day, no one would know how to appreciate that deed. Getting rid of the metric system was also convenient for merchants, since they were fully aware of the malleability of the usual measurements and the advantages that this represented. A few interpreted this resistance as the *Tultecos'* mere rejection of anything that came from the capital, just as we had rejected the anthem. So we continued measuring as we always had, and long afterward, when an inspector was sent from the General Management of Weights and Measures, Maradiaga led him into his office and gave him a paper bag. What's inside, he told him, is worth the same if we measure it in pesos, dollars, or shillings.

POOR DEVILS, I THOUGHT. From a bench in the plaza I observed the swarm of employees in the sun, with their stifling ties, grasping their briefcases tightly because someone had told them that the city was full of thieves. Everyone seemed to be hurrying somewhere, toward the building covered with mirrors, toward the bus about to depart, toward the meeting with Mr. So-and-So who promised to sign today, toward the parking lot because in five minutes they would be charged for another hour. Now I am no more than a spectator of that world. I stopped at the bench and said, "Cheers," to a group of office workers with my bottle of orangeade. Poor devil, they must have thought. I, too, had hurried like them to get to a meeting. We would sit around a table, and after closing the door, the outside world disappeared. No one could leave until it was determined why machine number twelve was producing polyester with a viscosity 2 percent lower than standard. At that moment, nobody believed in God or missed his children or remembered the high blood pressure diagnosed by his doctor: nothing existed except for machine number twelve and the 2 percent.

Two young girls walked by, secretaries maybe. I looked for Carmen in their eyes. Nothing. This is what I inherited from the *viejo* Capistrán: a way of carefully observing all women to see what I find in them. Across from me a woman parked her pushcart with its canvas top and set out a large selection of imported chocolates. To the right, a man with no left arm spread out a blanket on which he piled up different regional sweets. The customers preferred the woman; the man was surrounded only by flies.

And if that woman were Carmen? Why have I only been looking for her in attractive, young women? Why could she not be an old lady with thick, dry skin, a hairy chin, and a bitter voice that yells, "Chocolates, chocolates," like someone would shout insults to the passersby. Carmen with her dirty handkerchief around her neck, with the greenish nail that sticks out of her huarache, with her breasts toppling over onto her stomach. Carmen saying, "One thousand five hundred," to whoever asked the price, jingling the coins from the sales and again yelling, "Chocolates, chocolates."

Irritated, I bought a sweet with flies and headed toward the fountain to listen to the trickling of the water. From there I could see cashiers ("I only have small bills"), saleswomen ("This price is good until the end of the month"), and more secretaries ("With sugar or without?").

The cathedral chimed the hour when the sidewalks grew crowded with schoolchildren.

My tenth day in the plaza was coming to an end, and Carmen had not appeared anywhere.

I bumped into a garbage can and threw out the candy.

THE NEWS REACHED the Hacienda del Chapulín the next day. At breakfast the señora commented:

"I heard that Juanito went into the Cave of the Rattlesnakes."

"Who?" Carmen asked.

"Juanito Capistrán, Doña Esperanza's grandson."

"Ah, the one with the iguana tongue."

"No, *mija,* no one talks about that anymore."

"Well, I think—"

"And what happened to him?" the señor interrupted as he spooned salsa over his scrambled eggs.

"Well, the only thing that could have happened to him."

They did not speak anymore about the matter, nor did they say any words to sympathize with Juan or Buenaventura. Carmen finished off her coffee and picked up the pot to pour herself some more.

"No, *mija*, I gave you permission to have one."

She did not contradict her mother nor did she look angry. She put the napkin on the table, excused herself, and went up to her room. There she read the letter again and, thrilled, wondered when Doménico would come to steal her heart.

Today I saw Carmen.

Carmen.

Carmen.

Carmen.

Carmen.

Carmen.

Carmen.

Carmen.

Writing it a hundred times would not be enough. I need to talk to someone. I couldn't even think of talking to Patricia. "You know what? Today I saw a woman that made me ache inside," and that would be the end of peace in this house. My former coworkers would ask me about her legs, buttocks, waist, tits, and face. And I don't blame them: Those are reasonable questions for anyone who has not found Carmen. David has great respect for Patricia, so he would be a jerk and tell me, "Forget that woman, pretend you never saw her."*

I will have to see the *viejo* Capistrán again.

*It's true; that's what I would have told him. (D. T.)

THE NEW ERA IS HERE. Or so the headline of *El Tulteco* prayed the day the telegraph was installed, with its tall, skinny poles that at first made the city look so ugly but were later not even noticed. These cables, or wires, the technicians explained, stretch from here to the capital, and they distributed a paper that listed all the cities with which Tula had been connected and was now able to send messages to, just as if they were a stone's throw away. Some people were afraid of the poles and tried not to go near them because, they said, if you touch them you die. All this was because one rainy morning the baker was found at the foot of a pole, cold, stiff, and with his hair singed. It was a lightning bolt, the technicians said, didn't you hear all the thunder last night? But the skepticism of most forced the technicians to climb up to the top and take the wires in their bare hands. Look, they said, it's not dangerous. And even though as time went by most learned to see the telegraph as a good and inoffensive thing, the habit of speeding up when walking underneath the cables persisted. With everything ready to send the first messages, the matter was delayed two weeks while the governors of Tamaulipas and San Luis reached an agreement on the date and time of the inauguration. Finally, one Saturday, General Arizpe arrived in Tula and without formalities or speeches headed for the telegraph office. They spent a few minutes sending each other messages about the greatness of the event and Arizpe read out loud what he had received from San Luis. Governor Camargo says that modernization shortens the distances. Applause could be heard and after a while he read another note: he says that science should be at the service of peace, and more applause. Things began to deteriorate because some señoras wanted to show off the virtues of the device. Send a greeting to Chito Vázquez, he works in the slaughterhouse there. Tell my husband to come back soon because Polito is sick to his stomach. And since Arizpe refused to serve as messenger, the people thought that it was all a farce and that the device did nothing more than make chirping noises. The two governors were saying good-bye when the one in San Luis sent one final message: **AN EPIDEMIC OF YELLOW FEVER IS DECLARED WE ARE TAKING THE NECESSARY MEASURES.** Doña Esperanza was frightened, thinking about Teté, and General Arizpe, as if nothing had happened, took his carriage back to Victoria. The technicians packed up their equipment and headed off to where they would put other new installations. Only the man versed in the language of dots and dashes stayed behind, and according to him, only until he had taught someone else how to do it.

"I DIDN'T THINK YOU WERE going to come back."

The warm and desperate tone of his voice made me certain that he would not have let another day go by without calling me.

"Well, here I am," I said, thinking it a better idea not to say anything.

"What have you been up to?"

Only two weeks had gone by without our seeing each other, and he welcomed me as if it had been several months. We hugged each other warmly and I even thought he wanted to kiss me on the cheek. This reunion would have been absurd even on television. I told him that I was still writing and I asked him for certain facts that were necessary to finish off a few passages. He did not seem to be interested in my questions, and if he did respond to any, it was with irrelevant and disconnected words.

"You saw her, right?" the old man suddenly asked.

"Who?" I knew immediately whom he was referring to. The encounter with Carmen was written all over my face, but I was embarrassed to be so obvious. I counted the beams in the ceiling: there were seventeen. If only there had been a thousand.

It happened at a public reading in which several writers, including me, participated. I read the excerpt where Doña Esperanza finds out her daughter is pregnant and the one about Fernanda's funeral. Every few lines I tried to look up in order to keep the public engaged. Randomly, I began looking toward different spots in the room looking to see who was listening to me with the greatest interest. My eyes slowly became magnetized by the eyes of a woman in the back row. My reading became more excited, and the pages were moist from the sweat of my hands. Then I read solely for those eyes, for that face for which I imagined a body, a history. I went through each line with so many stumbles, changes of rhythm, and such bad pronunciation that the writer to my right said to me, "Calm down, *compañero*, it's just a bloody reading," with such a lack of bashfulness that his voice filtered through the microphone and the people broke out in laughter that made me aware again of where I was. When I had finished, the applause was of relief. The secretary of culture began to talk about the efforts being made by the government to promote literature despite the budget's being "so affected by the crisis." The woman (the eyes, the legs, the body, the history) in the back row stood up and left the room. I excused myself and ran after her.

"Why are you leaving?" I caught up to her on the sidewalk waiting to cross the street.

"Because of you. I don't like to be stared at like that."

It was starting off badly; nevertheless, I intended to keep her there even if only for a minute. I could already see myself in a few years chasing after her in a wheelchair, down one of the streets adjacent to the home, and her saying to me, "Crazy old man, you're a carcass." Without further introduction, I told her that I would follow her home, that I needed to know where to find her later on. Her angry expression changed to an amused, almost mocking smile.

"Wouldn't it be easier to ask for my address? That's what people do."

"I didn't think you would trust a stranger." Not that I thought that, I was just looking for a way to justify myself.

She took a notebook and pen out of her purse.

"Don't write your name," I said, "your name will be Carmen."

"Ah, great," she said sarcastically, "and yours?"

"Juan," I said.

She tore out the page and handed it to me. I watched her as she walked over to a black car that was illegally parked. Its tail-lights disappeared in the traffic, and I wondered if the car belonged to her or her father or her husband or her lover or one of her lovers.

BUENAVENTURA'S CRYING wore her down, and those who saw her so sad for so long said, "surely he was the son of the *negra*," and they pitied her and felt somewhat to blame for not having dissuaded the boy from going into the cave. Now he was in there, bitten by rattlesnakes, a skeleton without having been given a Christian burial even if it was in the cemetery on the outskirts of town.

For months Father Nicanor had a recurring nightmare that made him wake up exhausted and with his eyes glazed. Juan left the cave every third night, transformed into a snake, and he slithered down the paths and streets, into the church and past the nave to the foot of the priest's bed. There he rattled with some indigenous rhythm in order to wake him. The priest woke up and shouted and beat the floor wanting to crush the snake, and there, on the bed, wrapped in the covers, he said one prayer after another until the sun had convinced him that it had all been a bad dream.

"Let's bury him," the priest said.

But nobody dared to remove his bones from the Cave of the Rattlesnakes.

"It doesn't matter," he explained, "saying the mass for the dead and burying a coffin is enough to save his soul."

"In which cemetery, Father?"

"Right here, in the crypt under the altar."

And when he was reminded of the law that had been passed some years ago prohibiting burials inside churches, he responded, "Yes, but that law is for health reasons, and there is no way that this coffin will smell or fill up with bugs."

For some boys it was almost exciting carrying an empty coffin. The funeral mass was said on Sunday so that there would be greater attendance and more prayers, and Buenaventura went back to her weeping as if the actual body were in the box and she had just learned of his death.

Doña Esperanza attended the mass because of what people would say if she didn't, but she refused to pray, she just moved her lips during the prayers of the others and feigned grief by lowering her face with a contrite expression despite feeling more annoyed than anything else, since she regarded the *negra*'s moaning to be in bad taste. She spotted Pisco in the crowd, dressed elegantly in a dark uniform with gold buttons, and she couldn't help but feel old. She could no longer see the Peruvian as a prospect for her bed but only for the bed of her daughter. She made the sign of the cross and, as she left the church, felt envious of Don Alejo and Fernanda and of all the dead, but she was even more envious of a young girl with a thin waist who passed in front of her.

"What is your name?"

"Carmen."

"Some time ago I used to be just like you."

At dinnertime, when Carmen mentioned this to her father, he told her, "Oh, please, that old lady wishes she had looked like you."

They lowered the box in the hole and placed the gravestone on top. Father Nicanor sealed the edges with putty and thought that the usual prayers would not quite fit at that moment. He crossed himself, said good-bye to those who had followed him, and went out to his room. The snakes disappeared, and he spent four days and four nights making up for his lost sleep.

TODAY I WOKE UP with a doubt. What if the information Carmen had given me was false? I was so trusting that I didn't even take the precaution of writing down the license plate number, and with a false address and a made-up name, one can't get anywhere. I jumped out of bed and immediately took the paper out of my wallet. Patricia was still sleeping. The bedroom was in semidarkness due to the cloudy morning. I hurried out of the room and turned on the light so I could read.

Carmen
Maurice Ravel 147-B*
47-69-82

*This address and telephone number, taken from Froylán's diary, are mine. I don't know why he hid the real information, but I have proof (which I will not elaborate on) that my wife is most certainly not the Carmen to which my friend is referring. (D. T.)

The only thing for sure was that it was her handwriting. I had to trust that the information was true, otherwise I was left with two choices: chase after black cars or visit a handwriting analyst.

Those ideas came to me before seven in the morning. With the clarity of this moment, not only do they seem absurd, but they would never even occur to me.

I decided to wait until a reasonable hour to call. I had Froot Loops for breakfast and got into the shower. In the midst of the soap and the steam I found myself having even more doubts.

"Is Carmen there?"

"No, there is no Carmen here."

And what does that prove? That the telephone number is false or that I used the wrong name?

I came out of the bathroom, and after getting dressed hastily, without matching my shirt and pants, I kissed Patricia on the cheek. She whined, as if she were complaining that I was interrupting her sleep, and she rolled over.

My car started on the third attempt. Fortunately school is not in session, and the traffic moved easily, so I got to her part of town in a few minutes and, without hesitation, wove my way through the streets as if I had always known them. First down Insurgentes, then right on Pablo Moncayo, left on Felipe Villanueva, and at the end of the block the radiant sign: Maurice Ravel. I looked for the odd numbers on my left until I located the address just as I went over some speed bumps that seemed like the Great Wall of China.*

No black car.

She tricked me.

I stepped on the accelerator angrily, wanting to screech the wheels and blow the gravel off the street. My Datsun just barely

*Froylán is consistent in his lie: this is how you get to my house. (D. T.)

started, meekly, with no signs of anger. Mine, on the other hand, grew with each block.

Idiot, I said to myself after a minute. I'm an idiot. All of a sudden the obvious thing occurred to me: maybe the car wasn't there because she had gone out.

I made a U-turn and parked across from the apartment building with the number 147 on it, unable to distinguish which was B.

So as not to waste time while waiting, I started to write this:

It is 8:27 and I have the whole day ahead of me.

8:42   A boy around eleven years old comes out. He looks too big to be Carmen's, but who knows.

8:57   A woman in her fifties arrives with a paper bag. She must have bought bread.

9:17   And if Carmen is inside and it was actually her husband (or her lover, etc.) who took the car? I think about finding B and knocking. I lose my nerve and also think what an absurd scene that would be. What am I going to say to her? That I came to spy on her? I need a good reason to knock on that door, and right now I can't think of one.

9:23   The idea that Carmen might come out and find me here terrifies me. Even worse, she could have been watching me for some time through one of those windows.

9:25   I start my car and put it in reverse so I can park a half block away. From here I can see without being seen.

10:00 People have come and gone. The building is three stories tall. The roof is tile and one of the walls looks stained from the humidity. The apartment in the middle on the ground floor is painted red and clashes with the others. The neighbors must surely have a problem with him.

10:23 I'm hungry.

10:29 General Pisco crumpled up the letter into a tight ball and kicked it with his finger. Can you kick with your finger? Why not. It's the only verb that gives the exact idea of the action. He plunged a cup into the sink and took one, two, three mouthfuls. He was only concerned about his breath.

10:44 Here comes a black car. It must be her. It parks. I see Carmen get out, her hair pulled back in a ponytail. She is wearing a sweatshirt, shorts, and tennis shoes. She hurries up to her apartment because a man on the street is saying something saucy to her. Right now I am thinking about breaking his teeth, but then I forgive him since, in his shoes, I myself would have done the same.

10:47 Luckily she didn't go into the red one.

10:50 I am thinking about her legs.

10:55 I give myself one more opportunity to find a reason that justifies appearing at her door.

11:14 I start my Datsun and return home.

GENERAL PISCO crumpled up the letter into a tight ball and kicked it with his finger far away from his desk. He plunged a cup into the sink and took one, two, three mouthfuls. He was only concerned about his breath; as for the rest, a man should not be too well groomed or go around smelling of cologne.

The letter was long: Doña Esperanza gave her opinion about the economic and political situation in the country, commented on the cultural activities in Tula, and asked questions about the military plans, because the newspaper had mentioned that the French had landed in Veracruz and also in Tampico. She also wrote a bit about her family and dedicated many lines to apparent trivialities about Teté's studies in San Luis. Pisco, nevertheless, with the experience he had gained in the military, was taught to read between the lines and throw out all that smelled of rubbish and absorb only the real intentions and truths. For him the letter could be summed up like so: Doña Esperanza had an unmarried daughter, property, and the best intentions to introduce them.

Pisco walked the distance, greeting those he knew to be polite and those he did not know because he may just not have remembered them. Some long-stemmed, yellow flowers, similar to sunflowers, were growing. They sprang up on the bare hills and in backyards, as well as in the plaza and in the middle of the street, until the May droughts came or some mule stepped on them. Pisco thought about picking one, but it was just a thought.

He knocked on the door with his hand spread open.

"Señora, Señor Pisco is here to see you." The duties that had for so many years been Buenaventura's now belonged to a chubby girl named Amalia.

"What a hurry he's in!" Doña Esperanza exclaimed in front of the mirror. "I only sent the letter half an hour ago."

"Do you want me to tell him to come back later?"

"No, Amalia; show him to the living room and have him sit in the red armchair. Tell him I'll be right down." She mentioned the red chair again as the girl went off.

Amalia did as she was told, and even though Pisco expressed his preference to remain standing, he had to sit down where she indicated. In front of him hung a portrait of Teté with an engaging smile, posed like a great señora coming down a spiral staircase, with a look without weakness, unaware of the suffering in life, which to Pisco looked like a creation of the painter. Behind him was the languid and gloomy portrait of Fernanda.

"May I offer you something to drink?"

"No, thank you."

The portrait of Teté soon bored him, and he turned his chair around in the opposite direction. As he waited, he was drawn to the painting that was now in front of him.

"Good afternoon, General," Doña Esperanza greeted him, smelling of flowers and with her hair staticky from so much brushing.

Pisco stood up and greeted her with a kiss on the hand.

"I see that you have turned the chair around, General. May I ask why?"

"I don't want to be abrupt, señora; it's just that I wanted to be sure that the daughter in your letter is that one." He pointed to the image of Fernanda.

"No, General. She was killed a long time ago."

"Forgive me then, it's just that . . ." He did not know how to continue.

She showed him to the door without saying anything, barely looking at him. They shook hands for a long time, like old friends.

"And me?"

"What about you?" Pisco asked, freeing his hand.

"Nothing, I was thinking out loud all of a sudden."

Doña Esperanza went back into the living room and stood in front of Fernanda for a while, sad, her memory flooding back to her.

"Not now, *mijita*," she said to her affectionately. "You're not going to spoil it for your sister now."

She didn't hear the knocking on the door. She was reliving the smell of alcohol and the torn dress, the belly growing bigger and the baby that nobody wanted. What's wrong with Fernanda, Mama? She has tuberculosis, that's why you have to go somewhere else until she is better. But I'm fine here. It's only for a little while, *hija*. And in the carriage a small hand with the nails bitten off waved good-bye to her.

She was shaken from her memories upon seeing Pisco sitting once again in the red chair.

"It doesn't really look a lot like her. The portrait was done from memory after . . ."

"Who killed her, señora?"

"Juan Capistrán, the son of the *negra*."

"Him? But I thought that—"

"The son of the *negra*," she emphasized.

Pisco moved away like a ghost until he reached the doorway. Then he turned around.

"Luckily the snakes killed him."

And the woman nodded.

"All right," Pisco said. "I'll accept the one in the other painting."

Teté remained in San Luis, waiting for a date to be set.

"And what really happened?"

"There I was until dawn came. Curled up, sweating, scared to death every time I heard a rattlesnake or a little stone move. They were there. I didn't know how many, but I didn't care if it was only one. One could have bitten me just as easily, and what chance would a cadaver have of winning Carmen's heart? It was a matter of breathing as little as possible, swallowing the itch that was making me want to cough, and not opening my eyes, because the whites of my eyes could give me away in the darkness. The cave was not very deep and had a penetrating odor of brine and waste. The sun came up and I did not go to Tula, but rather to the watering hole to drink the sweat that I had left inside."

"If you were so afraid, why did you go in?"

"That is exactly what gave it significance: if not, I would have been taken for an imbecile who went into the cave because he didn't know what he was doing. At least that's what I thought at the time. I would have plenty of time to see the light."

"And was Carmen impressed, or did she think you were an idiot?"

"Next time you come," he said, looking past the window, "hide a bottle of tequila on you."

DOMÉNICO THOUGHT ABOUT letting a few days go by before returning to the city. The more dead they thought he was, the more merit his feat in the Cave of the Rattlesnakes would have. He remained hidden in the mountains, living off berries and at night looking at the kerosene lights that outlined the streets in the distance. He observed the silhouettes and the shadows, wondering if any of them was Carmen. At dawn, the city became invisible again beneath a layer of fog common at that time of year, until little by little the sun burned it off, revealing first the church tower and then the rest of the roofs. Depending on what direction the wind was blowing, Doménico could clearly hear the dogs barking and the voice of the *horero* announcing the time. It seemed like paradise to him: living far from any obligations, from stupid piano classes, from Sunday mass, from a voice saying you better do something useful; and at the same time being able to take in the comings and goings of people across a landscape that yesterday was his world and which had now become small and simple, visible with the radius of one single eye. He wanted to turn himself into a big rock that could testify to what had happened there over the centuries, but Carmen was down there, and sooner or later he would have to look for her.

He decided to enter the city by the street where the cemetery was to give the people the impression that he had risen from the dead and thereby give cause for the birth of a legend. Since this was not the usual route, he had to make a detour of several leagues through the hills and bushes until he reached the road to San Luis. There he came across a group of soldiers resting in the shade of the trees. Instinctively, Doménico hid behind some bushes. He heard them talking about how tired they were, how strong the sun was, the blisters on their feet, and about an invading army. "We're gonna be in deep shit," one of them said with the casualness of someone saying, "I'm going to the corner for some tortillas."

"Let's hope it goes well and we don't die," said another one.

The Cave of the Rattlesnakes now seemed like child's play, a pit filled with worms. Those men in uniform, with rifles over their shoulders, were going to confront an invading army, which surely had better rifles and powerful cannons, not little snakes that shook their rattles like a baby would. Embarrassed, Doménico remembered the letter he had sent to Carmen. He looked at the hands of the soldiers: tanned, with white cracks from so many calluses earned from their work with hoes and weapons. Rugged cracks that had the well-deserved right to find comfort in the soft skin of a woman. He felt his own hands, and their texture formed by the keyboard and water with ginger repulsed him. "Soft like a buttocks."

He thought about Pisco. Without a doubt he had not accepted

him because Pisco was just a decorative general, worried about shining boots, far removed from invading armies and the thunder of gunpowder. On the other hand, those men, about to give their lives and bothered only by blisters on their feet, would surely accept him. Doménico's excitement magnified, purified, and added distinction to everything they would do. If he saw them smoking, he gave their tobacco a significance similar to that of incense; if he heard them talking nonsense, it was the language of warriors; if the uniform looked worn-out and dirty, he imagined it as an extension of the scars on their bodies. He knew then that before looking for Carmen he had to follow those men wherever they went.

"Señores, I want to fight," he said without introduction as he came out of his hiding place.

"Not with me," one of them said. "Fight with El Mocho if you want to." He pointed to a man who had only the index finger and thumb left on his left hand.

"I'm serious," Doménico replied, "I want to be a soldier." Despite his deepening of his voice, the childish tone showed through.

"Thanks, kid, but we're fine just as we are."

"I think he *can* be one of us," said El Mocho, winking, "but he has to start by carrying our things. Then we'll see if he earns a rifle."

Doménico had seen the wink and captured El Mocho's intention, but he decided to accept anyway.

"Let's go to the captain; he has the last word."

And Captain Domínguez willingly agreed.

"What is your name?"

"Doménico."

"What a funny name. Are you Mexican?"

"Yes, señor."

"How old are you?"

"Nineteen."

"One more lie," Domínguez warned, "and you'll be going home."

"Thirteen, señor."

"Good. In this country the sooner you learn the business of war, the sooner you become president."

Doménico smiled, satisfied, and, almost without meaning to, pictured himself on a chestnut horse followed by a horde of fighters bursting, with gunfire, into the National Palace.

"Where are we going, *mi capitán?*"

"To Zaragoza," Domínguez responded, and noticing the questioning look on the boy's face, clarified, "to Puebla de Zaragoza."

The boy's question remained intact. Doménico took a sack and threw it over his shoulder. At the sound of the captain's voice he began to walk with the rest of the troops, trying not to fall behind.

As I passed by the cemetery on the way home, I thought about Patricia, Capistrán, and Carmen; about the piano academy and the Hacienda del Chapulín. On my right I saw that Pinez had written on the wall again in red paint. *Yesterday you weren't, I hope tomorrow you'll be.* I hope so, I thought.

DOMÉNICO WAS NEVER curious enough to count or determine how many soldiers were in the squad, as he regarded only El Mocho and Gonzalo to be his traveling companions, his colleagues of war against an enemy that did not speak Spanish; and the language factor seemed most noticeable to him. Where might those unintelligible men come from, men who upon being hit by a bullet and seeing themselves dying would use strange words to address a strange god. Pestraga bunto aquilmostorgo, Doménico thought without meaning to, and he imagined that to cross an ocean and forget about wives, mothers, and daughters, those men were surely very hungry for battle, perhaps for the honor of a woman like Carmen. Astropo milanten Carmentoga.

"And you, Gonzalo, why did you become a soldier?"

"It's the devil's fault."

"Do you believe in those things?"

"Why not? When they came to the hacienda where I was working to recruit, we decided to leave it to chance. We played a game of *lotería*, and I needed only the devil to win, but that card never came up.

The rest of the soldiers didn't pay the slightest attention to Doménico, except to make fun of his name.

"What was your damn mother thinking?" one of them said to him.

"Don't worry," said another, "I had a relative named Winstrimundo."

The boy kept walking without responding to the jokes, without complaining or even grimacing because of his legs, which were about to give out, his bloody feet, and his crushed back, with his mind tempted to recall happily the afternoons of piano underneath the shade of the academy's roof and the soft bed at night. At that moment he didn't give a damn what Carmen thought about his manliness. He wanted to throw himself on the ground and say, "Señores, see you later," but he kept on walking, and what he said was something very different.

"How much farther is it to Puebla?"

And the answers came without answering.

"In a little while."

"What? You're tired already?"

"Farther."

"One of these days."

"Don't give up."

"What's your hurry?"

Doménico would spot a tree far away, or a stone for a landmark, and he would say to himself, "Just to there." And as soon as he reached his goal, he would look for another tree or landmark and would repeat, "Just . . ." Then he realized that will is limited by memory and perspective. "If I weren't thinking about how much is left and I were to forget the last step," he reasoned, "I could always take one more." And so he continued for several days, convincing himself that the next step would be the first and the last until, in front of a hut concealed by the night, he heard Domínguez's voice.

"We won't move from here until everyone has seen La Flor. I'm going first, and the rest of you can decide if you will go in alphabetical or random order."

Alvarez, Cantú, and Díaz voted for alphabetical order; Salinas, Torres, and Villareal for random.

"If we respect the rules of La Flor," El Mocho said, "a half hour each one and ten hours of rest per day, then we can take leave for three or four days."

The will of the Zamoras triumphed, and a drawing was organized with numbered slips of paper.

"What did you get, Doménico?"

"Twenty-one."

"Give it to me, have a heart, after all you are still so young."

"No."

Several of them asked for his number with the same excuse, his youth. He just shook his head no again and again, hour after hour, until number twenty came out.

"You're next."

Doménico went in quickly, knowing that number twenty-two would be counting every minute. He closed the door and remained impassive for a while, looking at La Flor naked.

"Good evening, señora."

"Come in, muchacho, take your clothes off and lie down here."

"No, señora," he responded, still without moving away from the door, "I just want you to rub my feet."

He took off his shoes and sat down next to the woman. She took his feet and caressed them for a long time. She pressed the soles and the insteps, stretched the toes, cracked the joints, and even spit on her hands to simulate the softness of a lotion.

"For the first time I see that men have feet, too."

He remained quiet, watching her thick, yellowed skin like raw dough, her thighs like cones, so fat on top and thin near the knee, her breasts hanging down like bladders full of water and her belly drooping, with the crowning touch in the middle, a big belly button, black with dirt from never being washed. He looked at her for a long time, down to the smallest detail, and hoped with all his heart that Carmen, naked, was something else.

THE DOOR TO 147-B OPENED. That was the proof that, incredibly, after days of gathering my courage, I had dared to ring the bell.

"Hi," I said with my hands in my pockets, rocking back and forth to the rhythm of a bizarre dance, like a child who has to go to the bathroom.

Carmen looked at me without the slightest change in her expression. She didn't recognize me, I thought. I, unable to sleep for the thought of her, and she, waiting for the stranger to say something like "May I use your phone?" or "Can I wash your car?" or simply "Excuse me, I have the wrong house."

"Don't you remember me?" I had a hundred better options and yet I resorted to that schoolboy line.

The ring on her left hand was too ordinary, a ring for any occasion. I looked to the back of the apartment in search of a tie, an electric razor, a wedding portrait, some men's shoes. Nothing, not one single piece of evidence in sight. Maybe, if I could go into the bedroom, by the size of the bed . . .

"I want you." Did I really say that? Just like that, all at once? Or did I just think it? Maybe a longer sentence was cut short: I want you to tell me such and such or I want you to know this or that.

I was waiting for the door to slam in my face, but she began to laugh.

"Are you crazy?" she asked, smiling.

"Yes, I think so."

And as I was preparing an apology that would serve as a farewell, she said, "Good, because I am, too."

IT HAD BEEN MORE than a month since he had joined the Army of the Center, under the command of General Comonfort, and almost a month of listening to the thunder of the cannons in Puebla as one who hears the fireworks on the feast of a patron saint. The war was no more than an intermittent noise, since neither by stretching their necks nor by climbing a hill did they spot General Ortega's Army of the East, which was actually fighting. For Doménico, Puebla was a mysterious destination, of bells without bell towers, of trenches and parapets, of walls with holes, which was pointed out to him so he would know where it was. "Beyond the Popocatépetl." And he saw only the sun-touched snow and a green and disappearing horizon. They continuously received messages from the besieged city explaining just how distressing the situation was: food is running out, weapons, too; the enemy is advancing inexorably, although every meter is costing many lives. The will is still strong, but the battle won't be won with that. When, Comonfort? General Ortega asked, and Comonfort said that they had to wait for orders from the Supreme Government, that until then they could not give their support even if the city was taken along with the blood of all the townspeople. And as the guns of the Army of the Center grew rusty, propped up against trees, General Ortega's supplies were consumed with the speed of a fired bullet. Doménico, immersed in impatience, walked back and forth snorting like a sick bull.

"Why don't we advance and break those Frenchmen's heads open?"

El Mocho turned around to look at him. El Mocho was passing the time cutting his toenails with a butcher knife. After feeling the weight of his friend's stare for a while, he decided to respond.

"Because the government prefers to fight a foreign army and not against some general turned hero. You've seen what happened to poor General Zaragoza."

"What?" the boy asked, sitting down on the ground cross-legged.

"Well, they say he died because he was sick, but I think they killed him. Just imagine if they gave him the opportunity to pulverize the French twice. No, Doménico, there are some things that are not allowed in this country."

All the days were the same: stretch in the morning, sometimes wash the uniform in the creek, drill practice, become alarmed because someone who turns out to be no one approaches, drink a bit of pulque at night, and fall asleep, snoring. Until Captain Domínguez asked for a band of Indians to secretly transport ninety sacks of flour into Puebla.

"I have carried sacks all the way from Tula," Doménico said to the captain, "so I have the right to be included in the mission."

The chance to act had finally come, to get closer to the battle, to see the land bathed in blood, the wails of the dying, life hanging on good or bad aim.

What's more, Doménico was certain that those sacks were not filled with flour.

IT HAPPENED SHORTLY after the telegraph was installed. Since many people in Tula were concerned about the epidemic, many messages were sent to San Luis inquiring about the health of friends and family members, until a telegram arrived from the Ministry of Health: **THERE WAS NO EPIDEMIC ONLY ISOLATED CASES.** Those words were calming, and they were fine as long as one of the family members didn't turn out to be one of those isolated cases. Doña Esperanza was not a woman who made do with messages; she preferred solutions straight from the source, and so she sent a few words to Teté: **COME HOME IMMEDIATELY.** She called for Pisco and told him that now they could set the date. You choose, she conceded, although I would like it to be on my saint's day. Just assure me that you did not get married in Colombia. In Peru, señora. Can you assure me? Of course, señora. Then when? And Pisco responded, you set the date. Saint Esperanza's Day was still four months away, so there was no rush to make plans. Two days later there was a knock on the door. The telegraph boy handed over an envelope. **YESTERDAY WE SENT REMAINS OF YOUR DAUGHTER WE EXPRESS OUR CONDOLENCES.** As soon as the boy left, Pisco arrived, so caught up in frivolities that he did not notice the statuelike appearance of Doña Esperanza, motionless in front of Teté's portrait; motionless but being torn to pieces on the inside, on the verge of falling apart. The right thing would be to get married at midday to have the entire afternoon and evening afterward. The woman collapsed and even though Pisco saw the ground stop her with a sharp jolt, she continued to fall through a bottomless well. That's why, when she received the remains, which had been properly embalmed with a note explaining the health regulations with respect to moving a corpse when there is the risk of an epidemic, she drank a bottle of creosol, and Isunza scolded her, saying what a stupid thing to do. He made her throw up, forced her to drink large quantities of water, and put her on a diet of corn-flour drinks and vegetable soups. She did not recover completely, and by the time Isunza allowed her to go back to eating everything, old age had overtaken Doña Esperanza. On the anniversary of Teté's death, after going to mass and bringing flowers to the cemetery, she tried it again. She invited Father Nicanor and Isunza himself to dinner. There were three different dishes: she served the priest a nice veal cutlet with rice and beans; she ate a pig's leg in pepper sauce; she served Isunza a vanilla corn-flour drink and pumpkin soup. So that you know how it feels, she told him. After the three had had enough, Doña Esperanza stood up and walked over to the cabinet. She took out a laboratory bottle filled with bleach and raised it to her mouth like a drunk with a bottle of liquor. Let's see, Doctor, she said, laughing, if you can save me from this. And again Isunza, more concerned about the enormous pig's leg than about the bleach, made her vomit, pumped her stomach, and repeated the diet. Here, señora, he said to her when she had recovered, from this I won't be able to save you. And he handed her a pistol. Doña Esperanza locked it in the chest of drawers in her bedroom and threw the key down the well in the backyard. She was frightened by definitive methods that would not allow her to call anyone, not even Dr. Isunza, for her last hope, even if it was with corn-flour drinks and vegetables.

THEY ARRIVED AT NIGHT, just as it had been night throughout most of the journey, led by General Rivera. With the sacks of flour over their shoulders, Doménico and the Indians crossed the mountain both on the road and off, between rocks, bushes, and trees, in the middle of isolated shots and without saying a word, hearing only a groan anytime someone stumbled and fell with bare knees onto the gravel. And so, like shadows, they arrived in Puebla on April 18. Their presence was immediately made known, and General Ortega came out in person to receive them.

"We brought flour."

"Go over to the bakery on Mesones Street."

He made a signal with his hand and everyone moved forward, followed by crying women asking for bread and who were accompanied by their children to make the scene even more pathetic.

A mother with a baby in her arms approached Doménico and said softly, "I'll give you good money for that sack."

"How much?" Doménico asked, not because the offer interested him but rather to know how highly they valued his honor.

"Twenty pesos."

"Not even for a thousand."

Then the baby let out a heart-wrenching cry.

"Please, young man, look how hungry he is."

And Doménico, calm, without even thinking about what he could buy with what the woman was offering him, said, "Stop pinching the baby, señora," and he continued towards Mesones Street.

Then a little girl about eight years old with a pot went up to him.

"My mama wants me to ask if you can fill it for me."

Doménico observed her hopeful eyes and heard the imploring tone of voice that was sweeter with each syllable, and even though he did not want to refuse the favor, he knew that it was out of his hands.

"Tell your mama that this is not flour."

General Ortega was giving orders in front of the bakery.

"Fifty sacks will be for the soldiers' consumption exclusively; the other forty will be for the people."

There were protests and insults, most in a low voice, because there were more people than soldiers. "So," an old lady rebuked, "if we are going to lose the war anyway, why do we need to maintain the location?" But even though many felt the same way, the words, once said, sounded bitter, like a bitter cowardice, and they were enough to send everyone home prepared to resist the French for at least one more month.

"Throw the bundles over there."

Doménico dragged his sack and leaned it against the others.

He looked around him. It was, in fact, a bakery. How far will we carry this farce? he wondered. Why did they need to hide the gunpowder and ammunition in the bakery? Why not take it directly to the arsenal? He felt satisfied with his answer that the mission was too secret to do the obvious.

The ninety sacks barely fit in the cellar. In the back a couple of boys threw wood in the oven and dragged one of the sacks to where a man they called Don Pepe had indicated. All the Indians had left after the promise of a nice pulque as payment for their services, but Doménico's curiosity kept him there. Don Pepe took a knife and cut the very top of the sack. Then, the two boys lifted it up and slowly emptied it into a trough while Don Pepe added water. Finally, the three put their hands in and began to knead it vigorously.

"Hey," Doménico said anxiously, "and the gunpowder?"

The three men stared at him in astonishment. They were not looking for an answer but rather were wondering, Who is this guy? Doménico burst out laughing when he imagined the future of the war with cannons that shot muffins. He left, cursing Ortega, Comonfort, and Domínguez and their mothers. He went with the Indians to drink pulque and drank as he had never drunk in his life, more even than Carmen herself had made him drink. And that's all he remembered until he woke up in a dark, quiet cell to the whisper of a guard who said:

"I'm going to shoot you."

"*PSST*," I SAID through the iron gate. I couldn't see my watch, but it had to be close to midnight. The street was virtually empty after eight or nine, as it was a route that led to offices and shops. Getting no reponse, I knocked on the window.

"Yes?"

"Were you asleep?"

"What are you doing here at this hour?"

"Look what I brought you."

The interior was lost in complete darkness, and if not for the slight squeak of the wheelchair, I would have wondered who was talking to me from the other side. I stretched out my hand with the bottle wrapped in a paper bag. The old man took it and fondled it for a while, as the blind do to identify someone's features.

"Cinco Hermanos," he said, maybe shaking his head. "Couldn't you find a cheaper one?"

"It's the only one they sell at the store," was my excuse.

"Well, to get courage, any one will do."

"Courage?" my curiosity asked.

"I need half a bottle to tell the end of my story to the tape recorder."

"Then we are about to finish," I said, disappointed. A car with a broken exhaust pipe went down a side street. The noise broke the small-town stillness of the home. It broke the feeling of the past that is experienced in everything related to the *viejo* Capistrán.

"No, but now you should know the end in order to understand the reason for all this. Or do you think that I need to tell the story of my life because of a mere whim or simple vanity?"

"Drink half the bottle then," I said as if giving permission, "and if you need it, drink the other half."

I heard the noise of the seal breaking as the old man twisted off the top, and then an "Ah." The smell of tequila reached me immediately, that same smell that as a boy I associated more with a hospital than with a cantina, and that is why even now, knowing how irrational those memories are, images of nurses stitching up a wound and fast-moving ambulances with their endless sirens flash through my head.

"Do you want a drink?"

"No, thanks."

"Well, then, just go."

I got into my car. I could see several traffic lights in a straight line blinking their yellow glow. What might Carmen be doing? I gave thanks for having found her in a beautiful woman, very much like the one I wrote about, interested in literature (or at least in public readings), and not in a fat woman who twiddles her thumbs and yells, "Chocolates, chocolates." My thanks were not to God but rather to something abstract that you can credit when you can't think of anyone else. I had another bottle of tequila in the passenger seat, a Tres Generaciones. I twisted the top off and started to drink. The night was longer than the straight street with its flashing yellow lights. I turned the radio on and caught the end of a song.

". . . hers is love, true love."

YOUR HOUSE IS WHERE you live. It is a pleasure to fill it little by little with furniture and other possessions, but it is sad to have to leave suddenly and forever. Everything was placed just so, the bed facing a certain wall, here the shelf with the candle, your uncle's portrait a little higher, and think about where you hang that sword, store those clothes, put those pitchers and the bell you bought in San Juan, which by just ringing it kept away diseases and bad intentions. And all this for what—to end up throwing it all in a sack as if it were ears of corn? Because now there's no time, as if a volcano were about to bury us; and the wagons loaded to the top move forward, dropping along the bumpy route whatever is not tied down. The mules walk with no idea of where they are going, with their languid stare, with their backs arched, about to protest, and even the children throw bundles with provisions for the road on their backs. What didn't fit was left behind: the grand piano, the cabinet, the dead, the certainty that every morning, upon waking up and looking out the window, you would see the same hill, the same pharmacy, the same church with the same song coming from the bell tower. The land about which we complained—It's so hot, not even ivy grows here; Look how hard the water is; Pure dust, *caramba*, this is pure dust—becomes all at once a paradise lost. Everything was divided in three: going to San Luis, Victoria, or Tampico. And likewise the families, the money, the memories, the stories to tell, were all divided in three. I could not decide by myself. Carmen's route, that would be mine. I asked many people to be sure of the answer. Victoria, they told me. Carmen is going to Victoria. I searched my house one last time. There was nothing that would be of any use to me. I did not even need my horse…

Señor Capistrán, you shouldn't be awake at this hour.

…or my wagon or my mules. I took only a chest full of flowers…

Do you hear me, Señor Capistrán?

…and some trembling hands about to risk everything because now there was nothing to lose.

Are you drinking? Don't tell me you are drinking.

Go away, Mother, leave me alone.

You're drunk.

Get out, Lupita, and turn off the light, it's stinging my eyes.

Give me that bottle!

Give it back to me, Mother! Don't take advantage that I can't walk.

Go to sleep and I promise to forget what happened.

Please, pretty little Mother, I need another drink.

See you tomorrow.

Mother… little Mother… Sister Lupe… Lupita! Damn nun.

WE MADE UP OUR PASTS. Carmen was born in Torreón, on an old hacienda that had been absorbed by the expanding city. Her family rented out the stables to a series of merchants who sold women's clothing, costume jewelry, electronic devices, and religious articles. The barn was used as a warehouse by a stove wholesaler. At first they lived well from that. However, after the merchants joined a union, they pressured them until they got them to freeze their rents. The main house was still inhabited by the entire family, made up of the parents, a chatty grandmother, and four children, of whom Carmen was the youngest.

"Are you hungry or should I order you something to drink?"

"I'll have a *vampiro*."

In the living room was a large portrait of her maternal grandfather with a watchful stare, as if he were saying, "Don't be so sure I'm dead." And even though her grandfather had been dead almost thirty years, they would mention him all the time out of a need to believe in better times. Carmen grew up amidst comments like: In the days of your grandfather there was always food in the house; When your grandfather was alive, everything you see, as far as your vision extends, was ours; Your grandfather would take me to the market on Sundays and give me three pesos of the ones from that time so I could spend them on whatever I wanted; Your grandfather . . .

"Should we order now?"

"I feel like having pork tacos."

"Do you think they sell them here?"

"Let's go somewhere else."

The salary that her father received in exchange for sixty hours a week at an insurance company barely covered the necessities. The house began to crumble, and it was an embarrassment for the entire family when some representatives of the organization that promoted the preservation of historical monuments sued them on charges of negligence. At that time, the once elegant house was in the middle of a proletarian neighborhood. Opportunity presented itself when the government offered them a large amount of money for it, as they wanted it for the offices of Prosedol.

"Do you love me?"

"Pass me the salsa."

"The red or the green?"

"It doesn't matter."

"Do you love me?"

"This needs salt."

In accordance with a provision in Carmen's grandfather's will, the profit from the sale was divided among the four grandchildren in four equal parts. With the money in hand, she suddenly felt the need for freedom and came to live here. That was six years ago. She began to work in a shoe store, but the smell of feet bothered her, so she took the money out of the bank and opened a notions shop on Central Avenue.

"Do you want another taco?"

"No."

"Anything else?"

"That's an open question."

"Should we go to the movies?"

"I only like going to the movies when I don't feel like talking."

"What do you want to talk about?"

"I'm going to tell you about your past now."

"WHY ME?" he asked as he massaged his forehead with his fingertips.

"Because you're a big mouth, that's why."

"Where am I?"

The cell was small, too small to sleep without curling up; it had a big, heavy door, reinforced with steel bars, and an opening at knee level for communicating with the outside world and for passing food. There was no bed, not even a blanket or some straw on the stone floor for him to lie on. Doménico had gotten used to the smell of confinement, to the dark and humid cold like a mine shaft, but he could not get used to the idea that his country would repay him so poorly.

"In the convent of Santa Anita."

"Of nuns?"

"Yes, only they were thrown out some time ago."

"And why did the nuns have a room like this?"

Doménico was not worried. In some way he felt that the execution was just a hallucination, like a dream from which he would awaken when the bells rang for the seven-o'clock mass. The only thing that troubled him was how real the man's voice on the other side of the door sounded.

"You say that I talked too much?"

"Yes, you were pretty drunk. You were shouting death to Ortega and to the liberal government."

"But I'm not even interested in politics."

"Well, that's what you were shouting: death to this one and death to that one. The last straw was when you said long live the French. It was then that General Rivera said we should kill you right then and there because you were a spy, and then he said no, that it would be better to wait for you to sober up, because it wouldn't be amusing if you weren't aware of what was happening."

Steps from boots with toe caps could be heard. As Doménico took in the sounds and sights, the sensation that he was dreaming began to disappear.

"This is a joke, right?"

"No, I wish it were. When my general ordered me to kill you, I told him you were just a kid. How old are you?"

"Ten," Doménico lied.

"You look older, but still too young to die."

"Are you going to head the firing squad?"

"What firing squad? We are very short on ammunition. I was ordered to take you to the mountain when it is dark and to use just one bullet. And if you don't die, to crush your head with a stone."

"And how much longer until it's dark?"

"Do you think I just came to say hello?"

Strangely, the door opened without creaking, and Doménico

went out into a long corridor. Then, worried, he could see the tall, corpulent man. At the end of the corridor he could make out the light of a candle under a crucifix. They walked side by side in such a way that, once on the street, they looked like a couple of friends returning from a party. When they passed in front of the bakery, Doménico looked at it angrily.

"Did today's bread go out already?"

"Yes, early in the morning."

They passed through several plazas and by several churches where, unfailingly, the soldier would make the sign of the cross. Why go through the entire city? Doménico wondered, and in those moments that fear allowed him, he thought that maybe it was to expose him to the public and to serve as a lesson to anyone who might want to curse the liberal government. But not even he was satisfied with that answer because nobody seemed to notice them.

They got to an open field and the soldier indicated for him to stop. Doménico looked at the soldier's trembling, sweaty hands and knew that there was still hope.

"Don't you think that this joke has gone far enough?" Doménico asked in a falsetto voice.

Since he had met Carmen, he felt forced to be a man despite what his years mandated. That is why even in front of his executioner, with his instinct telling him to run, sobbing and yelling, "Don't kill me," he maintained a false calm.

"Confess alone, because there won't be any priest," he heard the man say.

He imagined his body running at full speed searching for a place to seek refuge. He also imagined the soldier's good aim, the bullet in his back, and the grotesque groans before a large rock silenced them.

"You confess," Doménico responded, "because let's see who's

- 170 -

going to forgive you for having killed a boy," and he felt that the word *boy* was a terrible but necessary wrong.

The soldier looked at him for a long time. Two beads of sweat ran down his forehead, and his face had become tense. He raised the rifle and shot in the air.

"I was only authorized to shoot once and I missed."

"So now you are going to stone me to death?"

"Don't be stupid."

Doménico took off running before the man could change his mind. He ran, unsteady and panting, stopping only long enough to catch his breath and start running again. He was ashamed to hear the whimpering in his breathing, which sounded like the lament of a widow, but he accepted it because no one else but him could hear it.

The sun came up and he dropped to the ground. His legs were trembling too much for him to sleep. Little by little the trembling turned into a severe pain that completely immobilized him.

He did not know if it was luck that allowed him to cross the French lines without being detected, just as he didn't know if the execution had only been a joke to tame his big mouth.

AND SO IT IS THAT I am from here and have never lived anywhere else, except for a few months, when I was still a baby in
my mother's arms, in Tijuana or Mexicali, I can't remember. The
rest of my life was ordinary: school in the morning, soccer in the
afternoon, with the constant dream of playing professionally. In
fact, I would score the deciding goal that would make Mexico the
world champion—in the last minute of play, naturally. I would
dream about that as I sat on the bench on the sidelines, because
not even on my neighborhood team did I have a starting position.
Yes, a common, ordinary boy with raw knees, dirty nails, grades
just barely good enough to pass to the next grade, and a fondness
for street fights only if there were more of us than of them.

"Should we go to your apartment?"

"See, you do like to dream."

Those were times when a little intelligence and work were

enough to get rich. But my father lacked both of those things. My friends were moving far away from downtown to new neighborhoods, and I was left alone, without enough friends to make the eleven needed for the team. Food was still plentiful, although made with cheap ingredients, and when we talked about meat it meant fried pork rinds, intestines, or liver. At dinnertime we would also revere the memory of our grandfather, who, according to my mother, was the mayor and never stole a cent. And the pride with which she would say it sometimes sounded like despair, like the bitterness of an old maid bragging about never having given herself to a man.

"Do you like elephants?"

"Yes, especially those that have no tusks."

"Would you rather die of hunger or of thirst?"

"Give me another option."

Afternoons without soccer bored me so much that I started to read the few books that were in the house. After some five novels, three books on how to be your own psychiatrist, two with useful advice for the home, one cookbook, one about the prophecies of a certain fortune-teller, and another about the life of van Gogh, I decided that I could write a novel. It was merely a matter of making things up and putting them down on paper. The idea excited me so much that I stopped studying business administration and signed up for the arts. When my father found out, he threw me out of the house saying that he was working to support a future college graduate and not a typist.

"Do you give your address to anyone who asks for it?"

"No."

"Then why did you give it to me?"

"Because I'm curious about what happens after Fernanda's funeral."

"Did you find my novel interesting?"

"I only said that I'm curious."

I was in my fifth semester then, and I was able to get a part-time job at one of the local newspapers. I jumped between the different sections working as a reporter. My favorite was the red page, and the articles that I liked to write the most were ones about crimes of passion and rape. I then stopped studying altogether and worked full-time. Now, after four years working there, I am the editor of the sports section, and every time we publish news of the National Team's latest defeat, I think how they needed me to score that winning goal.

"What is the greatest test of maturity?"

"Perseverance I guess."

"Are women attracted to foreigners?"

"For the most part, yes."

"What do you call those who repair wagons?"

"I don't know, I imagine wagon smiths."

"Should we go to your apartment?"

"No, remember that you are a repressed rapist."

ELEVEN YEARS later Doménico returned to Tula. He came by way of the cemetery road, just as he had planned to do when he came out from the Cave of the Rattlesnakes, only now he was not thinking about being a hero. . . .

"I can't."

"You can't what?"

"Skip over eleven years just like that. The novel needs continuity, a thread that—"

"Novel? What novel? I ask you to write a biography and you write a novel?"

The old man was looking at me impatiently. With his hands tightly gripping the wheels of the chair, he moved it forward and backward until the blanket covering his legs fell off.

"Novel or biography, it's the same thing," I said. "It's just a matter of what you call it."

"Or of the lies that you want to make up. Can you assure me that you have been faithful to everything I have told you?"

I hesitated before answering. "Almost," I said in a weak, apologetic tone, and before he could protest I added, "You leave some loose ends, and all I do is tie them up."

"I can already see myself as a character in some trashy novel."

"Don't worry—"

"I want to see what you have written."

"But what about the eleven years?" I asked to change the subject.

"Saint Matthew skips almost thirty years in the life of Christ and you throw a tantrum over a few useless years? Don't worry, nothing happened during that time. Or what? You want to write pages and pages explaining how I got up every day, went to the bathroom, then to work and to sleep again? If that is what you want, write it, it's up to you. I was disillusioned with the matter of war after Puebla, and I went to Aguascalientes. I worked in a saddlery there all those years."

FATHER NICANOR'S FEARS finally materialized. For four months not a
drop of rain had fallen in the valley, and although the situation was still not
so bad that the crops dried out or the animals collapsed on the road,
various sacrifices were already being offered at mass asking the Lord to
send rain. It was a Tuesday, a few hours before the first shower of the
season, after many requests that had seemed to receive no reply, when
Pastor Abraham arrived. He knocked on doors and consciences; he said
salvation is now here, keep away from false prophets, and he went from
house to house selling his newspaper at a price that atoned for all sins. No
sooner had word spread of the foreigner's presence than the sky clouded
over and it rained for two days nonstop. It's a favor that the Almighty has
granted me, he said. And before Father Nicanor could devise his plan of
attack, Pastor Abraham rented an abandoned shed and began filling it with
benches and parishioners. The following Saturday a certain Brother Robert

arrived accompanied by three women, whom he said were poor widows under his protection and care. He knocked on the doors of all the houses and in bad Spanish warned that the final days had come, that they would be included among the 144,000 saved ones and should throw coins in his bag. On Sunday, Father Nicanor had to preach in a church that was only half-full. Those demons have come to divide us, to make us forget about our saints, to put our martyrs back in the bonfire. But the priest's anger did not incite the people, who were already captivated by the gentleness of the newcomers. What's more, the rainy season had arrived because of the intercession of Pastor Abraham, and some *Tultecos* liked the idea of also having three poor widows under their protection and care. The priest called on Doña Esperanza, Isunza, and Madariaga. He insisted that they had to revitilize the Immigration Council. Look for some problem with the law that they might have, or you, Dr. Isunza, look for some unpleasant disease, starting with that fellow Robert. The priest's efforts were all futile because both men were carrying papers. They have the backing of the federal government, Doña Esperanza told him, be thankful that they don't lodge a complaint against your church or you will be officiating on the hill. Finally he asked General Pisco for advice. Look, Father, what those men are doing to you is the same as if you had a wife and someone came to take her away from you, and that can only be settled with a bullet. Good, the priest said, satisfied, after having thought about it a while, I'll put you in charge of it. No, Father, it's not my old lady they are trying to take. Feverish he returned to his church. He had only fired a gun on one occasion, when he was chasing after a rabid dog, and with such bad luck that he missed and the bullet ricocheted and embedded itself in the leg of the *horero*'s son. The wound became infected and Dr. Isunza nearly had to cut off his leg. That is why every time the priest would see the lame boy go by, he promised never to take up a weapon again. However, things were different now: every week church attendance was down and the collections had dropped dramatically. Not only did those scoundrels leave me few people,

Father Nicanor said, overwhelmed by grief, but they left me the cheapest ones. This seemed much worse to him than a rabid animal loose on the streets. He went back to Pisco and said it's all right, give me a rifle and let divine justice be done. And the general said to him that it didn't work like that, that even for killing there were rules. The best thing would be a duel, only this case requires three identical weapons, and the only identical things I have are these three machetes. I, myself, can arrange the meeting with them tomorrow, Father, at dawn, behind the cemetery. And that is what he did. The father slept poorly, thinking about the crusades. If so many thousands of men were killed defending the faith back then, certainly now, in the middle of the nineteenth century, another two could go down. And if I am mistaken in my reasoning, he said in front of the images of several saints, then forgive me. The first news he got when he woke up was that Brother Robert had left for the north with everything, including his three widows, without saying good-bye, without informing his faithful if they were now included in the 144,000. Well, the father said as he headed for the cemetery, that simplifies things. There he found Pisco with the three machetes and the pastor with the four gospels. Shall I explain the rules? the general asked as he handed out the weapons. And when both said no, he added, and if either one of you has regrets, he need only shake hands to forget the offense. Again both refused. I regret nothing, Pastor Abraham said, staring into the eyes of Father Nicanor, but you know very well that one of the few things your religion has in common with mine is the Sixth Commandment, so don't expect me to raise my sword against you, and he relaxed his grip until the sound of the steel bouncing off the dust was heard. You call that a sword? Pisco asked, offended. The priest raised his machete with the blunt edge heading front, as if he were grasping a torch, and again he thought about the crusades and Isabella of Castile. He was just about to unleash his force on the pastor's brow when a doubt popped into his head. What will the people say if they find out that I killed a defenseless man, a defenseless man of God? He turned to Pisco, who was watching the scene, impassive, leaning against the cemetery wall with his arms crossed. General, can I count on your discretion? The general said yes, that he was only a witness, obliged by the rules of arms to remain quiet. A thump was heard, and the dust came flying up with the convulsions of the pastor. And I, only a few steps away, saw it all.

ELEVEN YEARS LATER Doménico returned to Tula. He came by way of the cemetery road, just as he had planned to do when he came out from the Cave of the Rattlesnakes, only now he was not thinking about being a hero or a legend. His departure from Puebla and his later solitude, wandering along roads with no set destination, had given him a lot of time to think about Carmen and to realize that to obtain her love he had to become a man, since at that time he was no more than a fickle boy, a dreamer who one day wanted to be a pianist and the next, a soldier. A boy who changes his name, who went into a cave and into battle to find out the difference between flour and gunpowder. A boy who wants to be locked inside with a whore only to have his feet massaged, who wakes up at night crying because he dreams that a big, tall soldier is crushing his head; a boy who constantly mentions the name of a woman whom he loves, he knows not why, while tormented by the idea that there is little chance she feels the same way.

He survived the eleven years working in a saddlery where the pay was as bad as the treatment he received, because he said to himself that the greatest test of maturity was perseverance. And despite finding himself in a vicious circle, he applied that same perseverance whenever time and reason weakened his memory of Carmen. So, the feeling that had sprung up inside of him at the fiesta of San Antonio turned into an obligatory passion, kept alive every night by his power of suggestion.

Time went by, and women began to seek out Doménico: invitations, flirtations, voices through the bushes at the saddlery. He never wanted to become intimate with any of them, except for Margarita. He had a formal relationship with her that he refused to call a courtship. "Friends, we are just friends." They would go out to have *aguas* or to the theater or just to walk around the plaza, until Margarita began to despair.

"You who are such a man, and you won't even kiss me."

"You really think that I am such a man?"

And Margarita, surprised by what the question could imply, responded, "If not, I wouldn't go out with you."

Doménico kissed her for the first time, a farewell kiss, and he packed up his things to return to Tula, hoping not to find Carmen with a husband, chasing after two or three children.

He rode day and night, giving his horse the minimum rest needed so as not to kill it.

He arrived at dawn on the fourth day and stopped awhile outside of town. He washed his face and under his arms and continued his descent along the cemetery road, keeping a prudent distance behind the priest and Pisco.

"Did you bring me what you have written?"

When I entered the room, I thought that he was extending his hand to greet me.

"No," I responded without looking him in the eye. "I have to make a clean copy."

"Don't worry about that." The old man would not give in to such an empty excuse.

"And what's more," I tried another one, "there are loose ends from the very beginning."

"Like what?"

"For example, what happened to the uncle that Fernanda was reading the poems to?"

He looked at me impatiently. "That doesn't matter. I told you that because that is how things happened, but it makes no difference if my mother had come from visiting her uncle or eating at the Hacienda del Chapulín or from climbing one of the hills. If you want to, erase it and write something else."

I shook my head no. "We have already begun that story, so we will continue it."

He pushed just the right wheel of his chair so he could turn halfway around. I could not have cared less about that uncle, but I brought him up to distract the old man.

"After what happened to my mother," he gave in, bothered, "they completely forgot about him. After a few days Doña Esperanza remembered her sick brother, but the gangrene had already killed him. They found a rotten, smelly body, with the hands broken from beating the ground in desperation for so long."

"Well, I am going to write that," I said, even though I really thought that it would be better to erase that beginning and have Fernanda returning from some unspecified place. "What I *will* erase is the name Doménico, and I am going to continue writing the story of Juan Capistrán."

The door opened slowly behind the old man, and within a few seconds, the toothless old lady appeared and made a gesture with her middle finger. I went out after her while the old man was talking about something that I didn't hear. The corridor was almost empty, only a nun sweeping the patio and four old people motionless around a checkerboard. I went back into the room. Capistrán was still talking as if nothing had happened.

"... I would give anything to go back to the name Juan, but for now write Doménico every time you refer to me."

"It's just that it sounds bad."

"And you think the name Froylán is so poetic?"

He didn't want to be Juan anymore, and I was beginning to be him.

I heard noises near the door and I took off my shoe. If the old lady appears, I thought, I'll throw it at her without any qualms.

But nobody appeared.

I picked up the last tape that the old man had recorded and directed a discreet good-bye to him, barely raising my hand.

"Don't forget to bring me what you have written," he said as I was leaving.

AT FIRST THE CITY appeared to have changed so much that he felt as if he had never been there. But that sensation lasted only a few minutes, and little by little he was able to join images with his memories. The differences turned out to be slight: a wall painted another color, the church's paved atrium, the granite benches in the plaza, and, of course, several new houses on the outskirts of town because Tula was growing. What had definitely changed to the point of being unrecognizable were Doménico's features, so different from those of the boy who left Tula, with slight scars where the pimples had been, and now with a thick head of hair from the back of his neck to his forehead. He was certain that not even Buenaventura herself would be able to recognize him, and that pleased him. He would keep his identity a secret so he could win Carmen's heart with his status of being new in town, since he knew all too well that women are especially attracted to foreigners.

The first familiar face he saw was Isunza's, and even though Doménico had never been friends with him, he felt like hugging him.

"Doctor, how nice to see you."

"Don't touch me," Isunza said, and kept on walking.

What he wanted least was to betray his emotions, and in the end he was happy that his anonymity was kept intact. With the next familiar faces he was forced to be more careful, and he said only good morning to Maestro Fuentes, the clerk at the post office, Madariaga, and a couple of schoolmates—who all responded to him in the same way, as if being courteous to a stranger.

He found his house covered with a layer of dust, something that Buenaventura would never have allowed: grass in the flowerpots and the farm tools lying in a rusty heap. His desire to go in was frustrated by a chain on the door.

"Are you looking for someone?" a neighbor shouted from the other side of the road.

"The woman who lives here."

"The *negra*?" the woman asked, coming over to him, and as Doménico nodded his head, she continued, "No, young man, she went back to her land a long time ago, after her son died. Well, it wasn't her son, but she raised him—"

"I know the story."

"Then why are you asking me?"

"I just asked for the *negra*." He had assumed his false identity so well that he called Buenaventura the *negra*.

"Well, I already told you, she left." Approaching Doménico a bit, the woman lowered her voice. "Even though sometimes the wagon smith spends a night or two in there. I don't like that because he brings women who aren't his wife and—"

"Where can I find the wagon smith?"

"On this same road." The woman moved her arm like a pendulum. "Where you come across a telegraph pole."

Halfway there he was tempted by the shade of the trees in the plaza. He bought some peanuts and chose a bench that had gold writing on the back: *Gift from Doña Esperanza Lamadrid to the city of Tula.* He made himself comfortable, resting his elbows on his thighs, and he began to shell the peanuts. That spot looked out at the front of Doña Esperanza's house, with its overhanging balconies and the heavy black door that, at that moment, opened. Doménico expected to see her, strong and proud, but the woman who came out, leaning on Amalia's arm, walked with short, unsteady steps, her head lowered and her eyebrows raised in an effort to keep looking in front of her, with those eyes filled half with hate and half with nostalgia. The two women followed a slow, straight line toward the church.

"Good morning," Doménico said.

"Morning," Amalia responded.

Doña Esperanza remained silent. She gripped the young woman's arm more firmly and quickened her pace. They had already reached the street when Doménico heard her say, "Bad weeds never die."

"It had to happen."

"Naturally. If the old man paid me to write, it's logical that sooner or later he would ask to read the text. I knew that all along, but it bothers me to have to show him my version of things."

Carmen unwrapped a piece of gum and chewed it for about ten seconds. Then she put it back in the wrapper.

"What? You're going to save it for later?"

"Don't be stupid." She threw it away.

I took her hand and we went over to the painted wall of the cemetery in search of shade.

"Did you make up a lot of things?"

"Not a lot, just what I had to in order to improve some of the weaker points."

"For example?"

"Did you already read the part where the priest gives the small medallion that says *Lord, this is your child, too?*"

She hesitated long enough for me to suspect that she had not even looked at the first page.

"Yes," she said, and I assumed she was lying.

"Well, that medallion didn't exist, but after all is said and done, it's not relevant."

"It seems to me that you made up a lot more than that."

"And why do you say that?"

"Who knows, it must be because I am getting to know you."

"And what if I did? In everyone's eyes it must be a novel."

"In everyone's except the old man's."

"His version of things can't be trusted either. Why can he change the story at his convenience and when his memory fails him?"

"Because he is the one paying."

"So money decides what is true and what is a lie?"

"That's generally the way it works," she responded, using the tone of someone revealing something new to an idiot.

She was beginning to annoy me. I had two options: put my bad mood on display or shut her mouth. I pushed her up against the wall gently and kissed her. Her back was leaning on the latest message from Pinez: *As of you, morning awakes flesh to flesh.*

HE LEANED AGAINST the telegraph pole for a while, watching the men who, with hammers, bellows, and chisels were working to repair several wagons and stagecoaches. The name of the company was The Grace of God. Doménico thought it somewhat heretical to give this name to a repair shop, so far removed from matters of the soul.

"Hey," said one of the men, his clothes stained with grease, approaching him, "don't lean against the pole, you might get hurt."

"Are you the wagon smith?"

"Everyone that works here is a wagon smith. Did you want to see the boss?"

"Yes," Doménico said with bits of peanut stuck between his teeth.

"Over there"—the man pointed with his finger—"behind that door."

Doménico crossed the yard, not caring about the muddy spots, for since leaving Puebla and Aguascalientes he had forgotten what a clean pair of boots looked like.

He opened the door without knocking and inside found a man half-asleep on a chair, which was leaning back against the wall on just two legs. Doménico recognized him immediately.

"Abelardo," he said excitedly. At that moment he had decided that he would reveal his true identity to him.

"Yes," Abelardo responded, putting the chair back down on the floor.

"You don't recognize me, right? I'm Juan, your godson."

"Impossible," Abelardo said, half-convinced, "you died in the Cave of the Rattlesnakes and we buried you many years ago."

"Yes, Abelardo, you got me drunk for the first time. We drank a bottle of Gringo Amigo."

The wagon smith would rather not have believed him, since now he felt open to the visitor's saying, I tricked you, you fool. However, he did believe him, that man in front of him was Juan, it was Juanito; he detected it in his eyes and in his gestures, in the combination of individual features that could be sensed but not seen.

"Juan," he said, and he went over to hug him, but when he reached him, he just stretched out his hand.

They sat down and, with their smiles frozen and their eyes wide, began to talk about everything that came into their minds. How have you been? And you? You're unrecognizable. You haven't changed a bit. What do you think of my business? I was in Aguascalientes. You don't drink anymore? You're not a strolling player anymore? It's really great to see you.

Until the decisive question:

"Why did you come back?"

"For a woman."

"Then you never should have left because I know of one who cried her eyes out over you."

Excited, he thought that Abelardo was referring to Carmen. His hope immediately seemed stupid, as he thought of Buenaventura.

"What's done is done."

"What you should do now is look for her or write to her; you have no idea how happy it will make her to know you are alive."

Doménico stared at him for a while with a piercing look.

"No, Abelardo, nobody can know who I am. To everyone I am new in town and my name is Doménico. I am telling you because I need help and I can trust you. If the *negra*—"

"The *negra?*"

"If Buenaventura has already cried for me, why open up her wounds to cry for me again? I already told you, I only came for a woman."

"For whom? For the same little girl that landed you sick in bed?"

"I guess she's not a little girl anymore."

"No, of course not, she even got married."

Die right then and there? Kill her? Go back to Aguascalientes? Hit Abelardo? Go to church and spit again?

"What's wrong, Juan?"

"Nothing, Abelardo. Why don't you take me to the cantina and we can drink another bottle of Gringo Amigo."

In the four blocks to the cantina Abelardo had the time to finish the story. Carmen's husband had been killed in a holdup during a trip he took to the sugar refineries in Morelos.

Doménico ordered the bottle and took a few drinks. The mescal tasted better than ever.

ON JANUARY 1, 1873, after the blessing by Bishop Don Pelagio Antonio de Labastida y Dávalos, the railway line from Mexico City to Veracruz was inaugurated. Among those who made that historic trip was President Lerdo de Tejada, who waved to the crowds that lined the tracks from the Estación de Buenavista all the way to the sea. In Tula, plans were initiated as soon as the news was received. Imagine, someone in the casino said, our city will be at the center of all the routes. Whatever comes from Tampico, Soto la Marina, Matamoros, and Monterrey, or from the United States or from Europe, everything will pass through here, but no longer on mules with their tongues hanging out or in dilapidated, squeaky wagons. Yes, señor, the best years of Tula are yet to come. But we must be patient, Madariaga said, since the construction of the Mexico–Veracruz line took thirty-six years, many more than some of us have left to live. Don't be pessimistic, the answer came, remember that the delays were due to the war and the old methods of construction used initially. I assure you, in less than three years we will have our railway. Some half-drunk men clapped and raised their glasses saying, cheers, long live progress, long live Tula.

THE MESCAL HAD completely evaporated from his brain and his veins. It was midmorning. Doménico opened his eyes in his old bed. He got up as if Puebla and Aguascalientes had been merely a dream, and he thought that Buenaventura would be in the kitchen preparing breakfast. He stood up and, with the help of his bad breath, badly shaven beard, and severe hoarseness, he returned to reality. Carmen, he thought to himself.

He went down to the river for water. Then he took a bath and chose the clothes he would put on with the care of a bride.

"Where does she live?" he had asked Abelardo.

"In a reddish brown house on the street that used to be called Progreso when you lived here; now it's called Lerdo de Tejada."

He headed there in a hurry, as if after all those years being a few minutes late would matter. With his unsteady hand he knocked on the door. First the peephole opened. The contrast between the sunny day and the dark interior did not allow him to see the person who asked him, with the lukewarm voice of a woman, "What can I do for you?"

"Señora Carmen?"

The door opened wide, revealing a girl who looked like a servant. "She does not receive visitors."

Fool, Doménico said to himself, she may have just become a widow, and I come wanting to talk about love. Why didn't I ask Abelardo? Carmen, I love you, and it turns out that I say it to her next to a coffin. Idiot.

"Who shall I say came to see her?"

"Doménico," he said, realizing then that he would need a last name. "Doménico Terragoza."

Terragoza? Where did I get such an idea?

"I'll tell her you were here."

He stretched his neck to look inside. The house was not well lit, but the furniture, walls, and paintings were full of cheerful colors, or colors that once were cheerful.

"Shall I wait for her?"

"No, señor." Her voice became more forceful. "Thank you for coming."

THE OLD MAN hurled the question at me before we had even said good morning.

"Do you love her?"

"Who?"

"Carmen, who else?"

I was still standing with my notebook under my arm and my hand on the doorknob. "Of course I love her," I was going to answer him, but why did I have to? Why did I have to account to him for my feelings? What's more, those feelings are not exactly of love but rather of necessity, of anguish. Once before in my life I had felt this same anguish. It was a few months ago: in a lottery my ticket had only one digit different from the number that won the grand prize, a prize that would have resolved my life. That misfortune, however, only affected me for a few days, and this thing with Carmen feels like the beginning of a life sentence. She is the woman who could completely resolve my existence, had it not been for that one digit that didn't match and that constantly reveals to me the fleeting nature of our relationship. A number, a cipher, a voice repeating, this will end tomorrow, this will become a burden that you will have to carry forever; tomorrow you will go back to your wife and your old job; Carmen is a lie, a fallacy as great as your novel, like your stupid dreams of being a writer, like the *viejo* Capistrán, like the stamps that your friend stole.* No, this can't be love, and nevertheless, my answer was:

"Yes."

"Oh, well, then we are on the right track."

"*We?*"

"*You* are on the right track," he corrected himself.

I knew that his words were insincere. Part of him was involved in all of this. It was his will that had pushed me toward her, and the names Carmen and Juan had come from him.

"By the way, she told me that she wants to meet you."

"Who?"

"Carmen, who else?" I got back at him.

He backed up his chair as if fleeing from something. He cleared the way for me, and I went over to the bed and sat down. He looked so frightened that for the first time I thought he could be a weak-hearted old man liable to die of a heart attack if he was excited enough.

"No!" he said like a spoiled child. "She already screwed me up once."

"And now you foist her off on me so she can screw me up."

"No, not you. The third time's a charm."

"What third time?"

---

*I would never have thought that Froylán considered me a thief. (D. T.)

A truck with a broken exhaust pipe roared by on the street below, drowning our voices. The *viejo* Capistrán moved his lips, pretending to respond. He felt like playing around with me, putting doubts into my mind, testing my patience. Then Sister Guadalupe entered the room with a broom and began to sweep.

"Keep talking," she said. "Just pretend I'm not here."

But there she was, with her two ears and a happy little tune, unconcerned that all the verses ended in hallelujah. She swept every tile and under the bed with the determination of someone who does that job once a year, and she finished by waving her broom across the four corners of the ceiling to remove the spiderwebs.

"With your permission," she finally said, singing even louder as she left.

"Permission is asked to enter, not to leave," I murmured, not wanting her to hear me.

The old man had taken advantage of the pause to fall asleep.

"Hey," I shouted.

"Yes?"

"Why did I tell Carmen that my name is Juan?"

His eyes were smiling. He came over to me and took my hand. His skin was cold like metal; it had a scaly texture and smelled of old man.

"You haven't shown me what you have written so far."

His answer was not an evasion but rather a pact. I could hide certain things from him, and he, in turn, could hide others from me.

For weeks Doménico attended every mass, certain that he would see her there. But he began to feel like a saint because of so many Our Fathers, mea culpas, and amens, and still no Carmen, not on Sunday, not during the week, not at seven, not on Corpus Christi. "Has she just not come to mass, or has she changed so much and become so ordinary-looking that I can't recognize her among all these women?" he wondered, worried by the possibility that he would find a face different from the one he expected.

Having seen him so often in church, Father Nicanor approached him. "For as long as I have been a priest, I've never seen someone as devout as you."

Doménico didn't answer; the priest's words amused him, and he thought only about his devotion for Carmen. Santa Carmen.

And without the tact of a fisher of men, the priest said straight out, "If you are interested, *hijo*, I can send you to the seminary."

He shook his head no.

"Or if you prefer—"

"Do you know Carmen?"

"Carmen who?"

Doménico clenched his teeth. The name should be enough. Why would she need a last name? People like her, souls like her, didn't need more. Do you believe in God? Which one? God González.

"Do you know her?" Doménico persisted.

The father detected the anger in the question and relied on his instinct to answer. "Yes, but she never comes around here, not since she became a widow."

"I won't come back either." Doménico turned to leave.

"You look familiar to me. Aren't you—"

"No!" Doménico shouted without looking back.

He ran through the church as quickly as possible wanting to reach the door, and the sun that would not wait forever. As he stepped outside, he heard the priest:

"Juan!"

He kept going without looking back.

ON MARCH 16, 1864, a girl named María Fabiana Sebastiana Carmen was born. Of course, with such a wide variety of names to choose from she chose the best one, Carmen, like my Carmen. Her birth was not very significant, nor was her childhood or her adolescence. But at sixteen, she was sacrificed to a man of fifty-one, who, in addition to looking at her like someone who doesn't want to share his cake, was the president of the Republic and would be so for another thirty years. That girl had become Doña Carmelita overnight, and she had also become our last hope for saving Tula. But she could not hear us. She lived far away, forgetful of where she was born, surrounded by luxuries and ministers and bishops, and in the spotlight of photographers, palace dances, and long live the General, el Señor Presidente, and the nation. We asked her to save our city and she bought us a clock for the church, as if we wanted to count the time we had left.

ABELARDO AND DOMÉNICO left the Lontananza clinging to each other so as not to fall. As they were waiting on the corner for a herd of lambs, being led by two dirty-faced boys, to go by, a girl went over to them and, pointing at Doménico, asked:

"Are you the señor from the other day?"

Despite the ambiguity of the question, he responded with certainty, "Yes, I am."

"Blessed Virgin Mary. I didn't think I was going to find you."

Abelardo thought that there was something between his godson and the girl, and he gestured as if to say good-bye and not get in the way. Doménico, in turn, made another gesture indicating that he could stay.

"And why did you want to?"

"My *patrona* wants to know if you can come to see her late Wednesday afternoon."

That night he woke up sober and went running over to Abelardo's house to ask him if that had really happened.

LITTLE BY LITTLE Patricia has turned me into a human being with no importance. Right now, as I write this, she is in the bedroom watching television and maybe thinking about me. All day long she tells me that I am not the same anymore, that I no longer say things to her like I used to, and she emphasizes the *before* like someone talking about prehistoric times. Before Christ. For me there is only After Carmen. Prehistoric is pre-Carmen, and Patricia belongs to the pre-Carmen. Now she is a memory that lamentably occupies a physical place in my bed, a memory that I sometimes use. I am not going to assume that absurdity found in songs and poems: I am not going to say that when I make love to her, I see Carmen's face. That would be stupid. Patricia is merely a woman deceived like many, or the resident whore who falls hopelessly in love. Although most nights she seems like nothing but a huge hand.

HE KNOCKED ON the door quietly, since they were surely expecting him. Incredibly enough the calendar from Villasana Press
had indicated that Wednesday had arrived. What difference did
the year, month, or date make, if near the calendar's border, or
almanac as Buenaventura used to call it, the nine red letters of
Wednesday sparkled. The next thing was to decipher the meaning
of *late afternoon*. Three o'clock? Five? He supposed that the afternoon began at two and night at six. "Therefore," he deduced, "late
afternoon begins at four-thirty." He knocked louder and blew on
the petals of the flower he had picked along the way. He heard
the sound of feet dragging. "Dark feet, big and calloused." The
door opened without hesitation, without the previous peering
through the peephole.

"Ah, it's you," the girl said, and she showed him into the living
room. "Wait a *minutito*."

Doménico sat down on a plush couch, pondering the difference that a diminutive can make. "Wait a minute" would have sounded like an order, an obligation; on the other hand, "wait a *minutito*" was requesting a favor to which he could have refused or, even, granted with a condition. "Okay, but tell her to hurry." Embarrassed, he saw the insignificance of the flower and crammed it into his pants pocket. "It would be all right for a young girl, but not for a widow."

An opened curtain gave the room the light it did not have the other afternoon and which, perhaps, it had not had for a long time. The portrait of a smiling man proved that at one time the house had been happy. "The dead smile again when they become skeletons." The walls were painted a pale pink, and one of them, next to the white grand piano, was adjacent to the hallway from which Carmen appeared, the Señora Carmen. Carmen in black. Carmen serene, without that sparkle on her mouth that is shown to guests even if just to be polite. Carmen, who said, "Doménico?"

"Yes, señora, at your service." He did not know where the devil he had learned that absurd figure of speech.

It's her; the same one.

"What took you so long?"

"You told me to come today."

"I don't mean these few days, I mean all these years."

Carmen unfolded a wrinkled, yellowed paper. Doménico looked at it from where he was and recognized his own words, the same ones he had written before going into the Cave of the Rattlesnakes. He recited part of it from memory, a memory he had thought lost:

" 'Learn this name that is not of a man but rather of a heart that sets out in search of arms and war so that you will notice him.' "

"Yes, and you finished by assuring me that the day I least expected it, you would come to steal my heart."

Doménico hesitated a while before finding the courage to say, "Maybe today is that day."

She walked over to the sofa and fell onto it as if she had grown too tired from standing. She looked down, then looked off toward an imaginary point.

"I don't think so," she said with a long sigh, "my soul has already died."

He thought of several replies.

"I'll resuscitate it for you."

"I will be the coffin of your soul."

"It's enough that your body is alive."

"Don't joke with me, the soul never dies."

It was she who spoke:

"Would you like a *cafecito?*"

THE TELEPHONE RANG and Patricia, waiting as always for that important call, ran to get it.

"It's for you," she said after exchanging greetings. "It's David Toscana."

"The stamps were real and I've even found an interested buyer," he told me as soon as I got on the phone.

"Well, sell them."

"No, Froylán, that is your job. The client is a gringo from San Antonio."

He gave me his name and address in English, which I didn't want to write down.

"Do I have to go all the way there?"

"Not if you want to undersell them to a collector here. What's more, this man will buy them all."

"Did he tell you how much he would pay for them?"

"Up to forty thousand dollars if they are in good condition."

I did a mental conversion to Mexican pesos and was surprised by the amount. But I was not ready to sell them then, at least not all of them. Those stamps are the only proof that the past that the *viejo* Capistrán is talking about really existed, and therefore, the only thing that gives substance to Carmen.

I thanked him and hung up. Patricia immediately came out of the bedroom to question me.

"What did he say?"

"It seems that they are fake and aren't worth much."*

---

*The day after our conversation Froylán showed up at my house and I gave him the stamps, but he wrote nothing about this. (D.T.)

"THEY KILLED MY HUSBAND on the first Wednesday of the month," Carmen had told Doménico, and she asked him to come and visit her every twenty-eight or thirty-five days to say the rosary for the deceased. In the beginning, he would look forward to those Wednesday afternoons with the longing of one who is in love visiting the young girl who has seduced him with her suggestive eyes, with her simple words, and with the way she walked around the plaza swaying her hips. Later it seemed like the expiration of a time limit, like those necessary doctor's appointments that don't cure anything but at least alleviate the pain. Appointments at which love was not mentioned; at which the couple would kneel down in front of an altar in the little chapel at the back of the house and say one, two, three rosaries for Alfredo's eternal rest. "He died in the middle of the road," Carmen repeated, "with no one to pray for his soul." And now the job of saving his soul posthumously belonged to her and to Doménico.

"In my opinion she has already seen through your foolishness," Abelardo said, overcome with laughter, with his glass of mescal.

"To the contrary, I am the only man she lets in the house. That is a sign that she thinks more highly of me than anyone, and I'm sure that one day she will completely forget that damned Alfredo."

"You'd better have a drink to open your eyes."

Doménico took the glass and emptied it with slow, short gulps, as if he were sipping a very hot coffee.

"Do you know what she said to me the first time?"

"No."

"That she received my letter and waited for me a long time, that her husband became jealous and tried to rip it up several times, but she always stopped him from doing so."

Abelardo was more interested in his mescal. "And then?"

"That is what gets to me the most: knowing that if I hadn't gone off to play soldier, I would be with her now."

"Who knows, Juan. Remember that when you left, you were just a scar-faced boy with a crew cut. She rejected Juanito Capistrán and then she built her hopes around a man who was a lie, who continues to be a lie."

A boy stopped in front of their table and asked if he could get them anything else. They shook their heads no.

"It's true, Abelardo, I am so false that every month I take her a flower and then I regret it and hide it in my pocket."

"And who is the false one? The one who takes it or the one who hides it?"

"I don't know yet; that's why until I find that out, I am saving the flowers in a chest that Buenaventura left."

"Isn't that a sissy thing to do?"

Doménico didn't answer.

"I am going to tell you what makes a man," Abelardo continued. "He drinks liquor, forgets the rosaries, and by fair means or foul, he takes her. If not, how do you think you were born?" He turned toward the bar and shouted for another bottle of mescal.

They paid and said good-bye.

On the way home Abelardo gave him the bottle. "Here. In case one day you make up your mind."

"No, thanks."

"If you let things go on like this, instead of seeing you as a man, that woman will wind up thinking you are some kind of a saint."

When he got home, Doménico put the bottle of Gringo Amigo on a shelf and next to it he stuck a picture of Saint Jude Thaddeus.

"Let's see who wins in the end."

MAESTRO FUENTES was seen more and more frequently drinking at the Lontananza. He was always alone because if anyone went over to him, he would start talking in one of those languages he had learned in Europe, and even though no one understood a word, the bitter tone he used in his monologues was obvious to all. Many years had been dedicated to creating concert pianists, many years gone down the drain because after the initial euphoria, the piano became just a hobby for the *Tultecos*, another piece of furniture, a task to keep girls from spending their time thinking about idle things or, worse yet, reading novels, and an activity to make boys think of something other than sex. They learned theory, a few pieces, the lives of the great masters, and then they left school to go take care of business or a husband. The best student had been the one who would turn out to be Carmen's dead husband, and his greatest accomplishment was only as concert pianist in the state's military band. Maestro Fuentes was losing patience, and if any of his students made a mistake while playing a piece, he would insult them and make them practice for many hours after class. In one performance, Maradiaga's daughter, who was ten years old at the time, made the kind of mistake that goes unnoticed by most people. *Estúpida,* Maestro Fuentes yelled from his seat. The girl kept playing, apparently unaffected except for the two big tears that she could not hide. Madariaga squeezed his hand into a fist and, with the utmost patience, waited for his daughter to finish playing, for the applause to stop, and for the theater to empty out. Then he dealt one blow after the other to the maestro's fragile teeth. After that incident, his school was empty. That is why he began to drink and to send letters to the government in which he would ask for one of the jobs they had offered him when he had first arrived from Vienna. But different men were in power, and nobody knew anything about this Maestro Fuentes. One day the din from the cantina stopped because the people heard Maestro Fuentes from his corner table begin to sing the national anthem to the tune of the Spanish composer. Poor man, one of the customers said, it won't be long before he shoots himself.

"You have never wondered who your father is?"

Juan was aware that conception by spiritual means was something that had happened only once in the history of man. Nevertheless, the idea of having a father was so foreign to him that he could just as easily consider himself the son of nothingness. He didn't even have proof of Fernanda's existence, and questioning the identity of that unknown man was beyond the limits of his curiosity.

"No," he responded.

Abelardo turned the bottle of Gringo Amigo so that the label was facing Juan.

"Do you know why I drink this brand with you?"

"Because you are cheap."

The answer strayed from Abelardo's original intention. He took out a wad of bills and, after fanning himself with them, called to the bartender. "Bring me the most expensive cognac you have."

"I have only a very good Spanish brandy that was just delivered."

"Then bring me that one."

They drank it, with the faces of someone taking medicine.

"Damned Spaniards," Juan said, "they don't know how to live."

A fly landed on the lip of one of the glasses and then flew down inside it. Abelardo covered the opening with the palm of his hand and shook the glass until the fly drowned in the alcohol. He took out a coin.

"Heads or tails and screw the one who chickens out."

"Heads."

"I'm tails."

The coin did a hundred pirouettes in the air, fell on the table, and bounced onto the floor.

"Tails," Abelardo said, satisfied, "you lose."

Juan picked up the glass and downed it in one gulp. He coughed a little. "It flapped its wings in my throat."

"Your father is the one who makes Gringo Amigo."

"Wait for another fly to land and I'll get my revenge."

"Did you hear me?"

"No."

"Your father is the Gringo Amigo."

"I didn't hear you again," Doménico said with a challenging look, his hands clenched in fists.

THE VIEJO CAPISTRÁN maintained a serious expression despite the lively sparkle in his eyes that revealed a smile.

"What are you laughing about?"

"Me? Nothing."

It was obvoius that he thought something was amusing. What had happened to the mournful old man from the last time? I thought about the possibility that someone was behind me doing something funny. To be precise, I thought about that toothless woman saying "Fuck you" to me with some obscene gestures.

I turned around quickly; we were alone.

"What are you laughing about?"

He finally relaxed his muscles and let out a nasal laugh. "I am picturing what your face will look like when we skip over another good many years."

"Like the eleven in Aguascalientes?"

"Maybe more."

"Don't mess with me, not now that you have found Carmen."

"Precisely: if I already found her, what do you want me to tell you? What we would do every Wednesday? If you want, I can say a rosary for you."

My only response was to pick up my notebook. I opened it to a blank page and rested the tip of the pen on the first line.

"Froylán, Froylán, what a pain you are." After shaking his head awhile he added, "All right, but I am going to go very fast and without much detail, since for me each of those years lasted only twelve days."

I moved my pen, writing invisible words, urging him to begin.

"You don't play the piano anymore?"

"Not since that day."

"You were a virtuoso."

"You're exaggerating. The one who really played well was Alfredo."

"Your husband played the piano?"

"He was the best in Tula."

"And you don't think it effeminate for a man to be a pianist?"

"Why should I think that? Don't be ridiculous."

Some Wednesdays:

"The señora says she is not feeling well today."

Another Wednesday:

Doménico stuck the flower in his pocket and opened the bottle of mescal. The smell of alcohol intensified in the heat of the day. In a short time he had drunk half the bottle, and as he was preparing to leave, he heard the voice of Saint Jude Thaddeus:

"Don't go."

"What difference does it make to you?"

He took a knife from the kitchen and effortlessly stuck it into the picture.

"It doesn't hurt, right? Nothing hurts you."

He fell asleep and awoke when he heard the *horero* announcing that it was five o'clock in the afternoon. He ran toward Carmen's house, furious that he had lost half an hour, and surprised not to feel the effects of the mescal, he stopped to ask a passerby, "What day is today?"

"The twenty-third."

"Not the date, the day."

"Thursday."

Crestfallen, Doménico returned home.

Another Wednesday:

"We've been seeing each other all this time and you know nothing about me."

"I know your name, I know that I like to be with you, I know that you help me make sure that Alfredo rests in peace."

"Anything else?"

"For me that's enough."

"And what do you know about my intentions?"

"I know that they are yours."

Most Wednesdays:

Sitting across from each other without looking at each other, they talked about the weather, the future, and the palpable present.

"It's so hot."

"It's so cold."

"It stopped raining."

"The year has flown by."

"The fair begins on Sunday."

"It doesn't even seem like Christmas."

"Did you try the little cream pastries?"

"A mosquito bit me."

"My hand is swollen."

Another Wednesday:

Halfway there, Doménico stopped. At the end of the street he could see the reddish brown house, where surely the coffee was hot and the biscuits already served on the silver tray from Taxco. "Today I'm not going," he thought. "I'm going off to the whores," and then, indecisive, he went back down Union Street, looking back over his shoulder at every corner.

Wednesday, the following month:

"Why didn't you come?"

"Because I was with a real woman," he wanted to say.

"I wasn't feeling well," he said, rubbing his stomach.

One Friday:

"The señora says it's the wrong day."

Every Wednesday:

"Pray for us."

Wednesdays of anniversaries:

"Ora pro nobis."

Another Wednesday:

"Can't you see that I'm in love with you?"

"Of course, from the first day."

"Then what the devil are you doing?"

"Trying to forget Alfredo."

"And when will that be?"

"Sometimes I think not much longer; other times I think that you are going to need a lot of patience."

One Ash Wednesday:

"What did you hear?"

"A cry. Let me go see."

"No, let Concha go."

A little while later:

"It was a little old lady who fell from her carriage; she looks as though she's broken a lot of bones."

Today Patricia said to me:

"If I didn't trust you so much, I would think that you were cheating on me."

I could only respond, "How can you think I would cheat on you?" and then I continued with an absurd speech about love and fidelity as I kissed her forehead and her cheeks.

I left the house, wanting to walk barefoot on the burning pavement or cross the street with my eyes closed or vomit all over myself. I knew very well that I wasn't going to do that. I lacked the same courage I didn't have to tell Patricia, "Here, read what I've written about you." I crossed the street cautiously, looking both ways to make sure a car was not going to run me over. The guilt grew with each block, like a fungus, like warts on my feet, hands, armpits, ears, and eyelids. "If I didn't trust you so much . . ." It must be her weapon to ruin me because she knows I am a coward. Because I may never dare to look her in the eye and say good-bye, because I keep waiting for some magical solution: a bare cable or a car with no brakes or steep stairs that have just been mopped or a gas leak or lung cancer or so many other ways that are not simply "Good-bye, Patricia, I'm leaving you for Carmen."

I walked down a randomly chosen street. A residential neighborhood with gardens, trees, and two-car garages, with speed-limit signs, speed bumps on every block, and servants watering the grass. I heard a voice shout "Toño, come here." But Toño paid no attention, and laughing, as if it were a joke, he ran away from the woman, his mama, no doubt, who being three times as old and three times as heavy could not catch him. Toño had something in his hand; I couldn't see what it was, but it was surely the reason for the argument. "Listen to me," his mama repeated. And Toño, with that same joking laugh, ran farther away from her and closer to me, without realizing it.

My guilt alone was enough for that street. Toño's was an intolerable excess.

When he was close, I opened my hand and, with all the strength I had, hit Toño in the face. He fell to the ground crying, incredulous. I picked him up by the hair and forcibly turned him over to his mother.

"Scoundrel," she shouted, and I was on the verge of shutting her up with another slap.

FATHER NICANOR SPENT the entire day putting ashes on the foreheads of the faithful. Pulvis es et in pulverem reverteris, he repeated over and over, his mouth dry, as dry as a day in February with its cold gale that scratches the face and blows away the leaves and dirt and clouds coming from the east. The women struggled to keep their veils, which threatened to follow the path of the wind, and their hair was unfaithful to any attempt at order. Pulvis es et in pulverem reverteris. Amen, Doña Esperanza responded without stepping aside to let the next in line move forward. Father, come with me to give ashes to my two daughters. Don't talk nonsense, Esperanza, this rite serves no purpose for the dead. But the hunchedover old lady was in no mood to listen to reason. Take me to the cart, Amalia. She took hold of her arm and let herself be led slowly to the carriage parked in front of the church. A fifty-year-old man helped her to get in. Where shall I take you, señora? To the cemetery. With an order from the driver, the two horses headed uphill toward the Cerro del Camposanto. Once there, Doña Esperanza got out at the tomb. Gil Lamadrid Family, it said in the middle of the granite tombstone, and then three names: Alejo, Fernanda, Teté. Above the names of each daughter she drew a cross with the ashes from a cigar. My daughters were dust and to dust they have returned. The wind blew stronger. Doña Esperanza held on to Amalia's arm so as not to lose her balance. Let's go now, señora, there is a lot of dirt here that might not be good for you. On the contrary, muchacha, shovelfuls of dirt over my body would be the best thing that could happen to me. They got in the carriage and headed back. Do you want me to put the canvas cover on? No, the sun is good for me. There were two versions of what happened next. The driver said that the wheels hit a big rock and that because the carriage jolted, the señora fell like a sack of potatoes. Amalia said that it was because she was dozing, and the jolt of the carriage came when the back wheel ran over the poor woman. She agreed completely with the part about the sack of potatoes. The girl let out a scream, thinking that her *patrona* was dead, but when they approached the body they noticed that she was still breathing, moaning slightly. Four men lifted her onto a wicker stretcher and carried her all the way to her bedroom. Isunza came at once to examine her bones. As Doña Esperanza was coming to, her whimpering turned into shrieks. Isunza put her to sleep with some ether and continued to feel her broken body. As there were no relatives, he came out of the bedroom to inform the curious: fractures of the right clavicle, both tibias, coccyx, left femur, probably all the ribs, and with some bad luck even the skull. He walked through the people, across the plaza, and into the church, where he found the father washing his hands to remove the dark spots that the ashes had left on his index finger and thumb. Father, Doña Esperanza needs the last rites. *Caramba,* she did it again. I don't know, it may have been an accident. Let's go on over there. In front of the broken body of Doña Esperanza at rest, the priest asked how long she had to live. That depends on us, Isunza responded, but the sooner the better. How is that, Doctor? You see, Father, this woman will have to be sacrificed like a sick mare. No, the priest said angrily, she's not an animal. In other words, Isunza replied, your church is more compassionate to animals than to human beings. No, it's not that; it's just that animals are animals and people are people. But such a poor argument forced him to reason things another way. He turned around to see all the luxuries that surrounded him, and he thought about the big house, just a few steps from the church, and he also thought about the Hacienda del Molinillo, the Rancho del Gavilán and its herd of cows, about the sack and rope factory, and about the mill in San Antonio. Then he took his implements of faith and administered the holy oil. All right, Dr. Isunza, do as you please.

"CARMEN, A LOT OF things are not the way we want them
to be."

She laughed. She was looking at her bottle of Coca-Cola carefully; I think she was counting the bubbles that were rising to the
surface. Then she lifted the bottle to her ear.

"Listen: even my Coke says more intelligent things than
you do."

"I'm serious."

"That's even worse."

She covered the opening of the bottle with her thumb and
shook it. Then, with poor aim, she squirted it, apparently at me.
Some women at the next table felt threatened and opted to
change tables. The waiter appeared with an angry look and a mop
in his hand. Carmen kept laughing.

"Next time I won't miss," she warned me.

"Listen, this is all a lie. My name is Froylán Gómez, I am married, and I have no job."

She shook the bottle again and showered me with Coke. Now she wasn't laughing, she wasn't playing.

"You are Juan," she said firmly, in a holy tone, "you work for a newspaper, the sports section, and you don't need any other woman than me."

I agreed.

I paid the bill.

Carmen insisted on licking the Coke off me as we sped down the road.

"Where are we going?"

"To bring a bottle to the old man Capistrán."

"Good, let's see if I finally get to meet him."

"No, Carmen, you'll stay in the car."

I parked a half block away to be sure that they didn't see each other and, almost running, reached his window and said:

"Here's another bottle so you can finish your story for me."

On the way home I passed the cemetery, without turning to see if Pinez had written anything else.

FATHER NICANOR SIPPED his tamarind *agua* and sat back in
the chair at his desk. His office reflected a coexistence of the
ethereal and the worldly: Bibles, crucifixes, pictures of saints,
hosts, a small basin of holy water, and incense, but also ledgers,
title deeds, and a walnut filing cabinet full of official documents,
bulls, communiqués from the bishop, and judicial orders. He took
off his shoes and socks and stretched out his legs, wiggling his toes
as if he were playing a harp. He had just buried Doña Esperanza;
a funeral in which the few who were present looked at each other.
These few found themselves hesitant, in search of someone to
whom they could express their condolences, but nobody was grief-
stricken enough that they could go over to him or her and hug
and say I'm so sorry. They lifted the tombstone with the smudged-
ash crosses and they lowered the body with the same briskness
with which she had fallen from the carriage twenty hours earlier.

Out of the corner of his eye, the priest noticed the door opening. He thought it could be the wind, a divine hand, an imperceptible slant, hinges with a will of their own. He did not want to think the obvious. "I don't want visitors now. Can't you see I am tired and my feet hurt?"

"Good afternoon, Father."

"Confessions are from three to five Monday to Saturday; arrangements for baptisms, marriages, annulments, first Communions, and benedictions must be made during office hours; mass schedules can be found at the entrance; the price for bulls for the dead is negotiated in the mornings; right now I am only attending to the dying."

"I didn't come for any of that," Doménico said, looking at the father's feet.

"Then allow me," the priest responded, and without reserve, he swiped his index finger through his toes to remove the sweaty dirt.

"I found out that you are going to be in charge of administering the property of the deceased Señora Lamadrid."

"Not me, but the Church," the father said, suppressing the comments that had spontaneously sprung up inside him: "And what do you care?" or "How fast gossip travels" or "But they are just some small lands."

"I think I am the heir," Doménico said, not knowing whether to be firm, irate, or pleasant, and he thought it opportune to clarify:

"I am her only relative."

"Juan Capistrán," the priest said, recognizing him. "Why did you come back?"

"That doesn't matter."

"And why when I called your name out in church did you pretend not to hear?"

"That doesn't matter either."

"Well, now you're going to have to work hard to convince people that you are the grandson of the deceased. All those who knew Doña Esperanza know that she had only one husband, two daughters, and a grandson, and I buried all of them myself," and upon saying that, he thought of the ants, the difficult childbirth, the fever, and the snakes. Which would have been the best death? He chose that of Don Alejo, since to die like Fernanda you had to be a woman. Teté's was purulent and foul-smelling, and snakes repulsed him. Yes, better with ants and drunk; in that way death is like a deep sleep.

"You also buried the grandson?"

"Yes," the priest responded with his eyes wide open.

Doménico told him that he had two ways to prove it. Two things that would prove that he was Juan Capistrán, the same one from the Cave of the Rattlesnakes, the very same son of Fernanda.

"That will have to be seen," Father Nicanor challenged.

Doménico stuck his hand into his shirt and pulled out the small medallion that said, *Lord, this is your child, too.*

"What does this prove?" the father asked after examining the authenticity of the medallion, and he answered himself, "Just that you are an opportunist who found a body in the cave. That you are a thief with no respect even for the dead."

"The other proof," Doménico said calmly, "I got by chance, the day I returned to Tula. You were with Pisco behind the cemetery and you dealt a blow to a man with a machete. Then I saw how you dragged him to—"

"Stop." The father put on his shoes and socks and silently walked over to the window. From there he stared at Doña Esperanza's house for a long time, its balconies, the white walls. He imagined the possibility of negotiating a deal, but he shook his head no and after a deep breath said, "Looking at it more carefully, the first proof is enough."

Doménico entered the deceased woman's house, went up the stairs, and out onto the balcony.

"Carmen!" he shouted, knowing that she wouldn't hear him. "I am Juan Capistrán again!"

And so, once again in his first house and with his original name, he decided to continue what he had begun that day of San Antonio, that which Doménico, in the end, had never achieved.

I REMEMBER THE DATE WELL. It was April 17. It was one of those days when the heat of the sun bakes you and the cold of the shade numbs you. We had just come through a very cold winter, the air was dry and the trees were still bare, providing only scarce outlines of shade on the dry roads. The faces of the people who passed in front of me were also dry. And I, leaning up against a walnut tree, watched the people drain out of Tula along every road. Along the road to Victoria. Carmen's route. Entire families went by, sad but determined to leave, because in the houses they were leaving behind, only solitude, immobility, and deterioration, like a plague, loomed. The desolation of the cemetery advanced toward the plaza, toward the school and the church, toward the bodegas, the haciendas, the hotel and the casino, toward the houses, including her house. And there I was, waiting for her by the walnut tree, ready to risk my life for a letter that now had no value. I spotted her carriage pulled by a chestnut-colored horse as soon as it appeared around the curve. It advanced solidly, in spite of its wheels that seemed not to turn. For the first time she was not wearing black. I put my hand on the chest and opened it, exposing all the flowers that I had kept for her every month. Yes… out of pity. Out of pity Carmen would tell me get in, let's get out of this place. She passed in front of me. Awkwardly, I stuck my hand in the chest to stir up the flowers. She looked at me with the sorrow with which one looks at a dead person. She did not stop to pick up the body, to throw it in with the baggage. The carriage moved off with weeping in its wheels. I remained up against the walnut tree until my legs couldn't take it and I fell to the ground, and from there I watched the rest of the people passing by, as if they didn't see me. The last one to leave was the priest. He did stop, and not out of pity but rather out of a holy sense of obligation. Let's go, Juan, he said to me as he got down off his mule. I couldn't stand up, nor could I ever from that point on. Father Nicanor went back to my house, got my wagon and filled it with what he found in the attic and finally, as if he were lifting a beast that had been slit from top to bottom, he lifted me up and put me in with everything else. I was motionless, paralyzed, without the will to go one way or the other. I am going to take you to the nuns so that they can take care of you until you can walk again, he said to me some ways down the road. Buenaventura must have received the letter and returned home to find everything dead and, once again, knelt down in front of my empty grave, inside that great grave that Tula had become; she must have cried until she fell asleep, without the energy or desire to wake up.

"Wait, young man."

The *viejo* Capistrán's room was locked. I was getting ready to knock when I heard that voice behind me.

"Wait."

I wanted to see a familiar face, but all the old people in the home seemed to have the same monotonous features, the same measured way of walking without hurrying. Not until he was near did I see the closed eyelid, greenish and concave.

"I'm El Tuerto."

I had already figured it out. "Yes?"

"Last night he got drunk and he has been very upset, that's why I closed his door. I didn't want them to see him cry because then the others, assholes that they are, make fun of him. Stupid old folks . . . it makes them mad that you come to see him so often, and the rest of us were forgotten long ago."

I thought he was going to tell me about the hardships of living in the home, but instead he said, "He already told you, right?"

"What?"

"About the day he left Tula."

I told him that he had.

"I thought so. Many years ago, when he was also drunk, he told me, and he began to cry like a baby and wouldn't eat for several days."

He opened the door slowly to soften the creaking of the hinges. I saw the *viejo* Capistrán in front of the window, his back to us.

"Come in," he said.

El Tuerto motioned as if to say good-bye.

"I'm already in." I continued to display my difficulty in initiating conversations.

"Did you listen to the last tape?" His voice was weak.

"Yes."

And still next to the window, as if it were the window of a confessional, he asked, "Do you think it's possible to keep living after that?"

"Well, you are still alive."

"No, Froylán, it just looks that way." He turned his chair toward me. Once again he was the submissive, fragile, and trembling man of our first meeting. "One loses the right even to die after looking for the pity of a woman, after stirring up some damned flowers, and all for . . ."

His head dropped, as if he had all of a sudden fallen asleep. However, tension was still in his hands and he was breathing unevenly.

He looked up and pushed his chair over to me. With his eyes sunken and his voice dragging, he bent over completely at the waist, in what seemed like his way of kneeling.

"Make things turn out differently."

Juan did not know what time it was when the knocking at the door woke him up, but he thought it must have been around four in the morning. He looked out from the balcony.

"What is it?"

A tall, old man with a foreign accent looked up and, not seeing anyone in the darkness, asked, "Excuse me, does Fernanda live here?"

He went downstairs and opened the door.

"Come in."

"I'm sorry for coming at this hour, but I've come from far away and I didn't want to wait any longer."

Juan heard a horse snorting outside. He looked out, intrigued, because he had not seen it from the balcony, but he was still unable to see it.

"What a dark night," Juan said, and closed the door.

"Almost black."

He lit a couple of lamps and the man looked about the house as if he recognized it, or rather remembered it, without daring to go upstairs.

"In this spot we danced our only dance; next to that wall there was a piano that played all night long, and right there, where you are, I promised her that I would take her far away."

"And why did you not come back until now?"

There was no reply.

"Does she still live here?" the man asked.

"Not here or anywhere."

With his eyes twitching, the man said something in a language that Juan did not understand and, after an unsustainable silence, began to cry.

"That's how it will always be," the man said with difficulty. "I will come to ask for her, and you, or whoever is here, will tell me the same thing."

Juan thought that the man needed a drink, and he picked out a bottle with a French label. They shared it like two old friends, each one taking a drink without wiping off the top.

"Do you know who I am?" the man asked.

"Yes, I do."

They continued drinking the rest of the night until drunkenness caught up with them. Juan woke up midmorning. He was alone, and there was no sign of the horse.

AT TIMES ONE FEELS drawn to the plight of the weak and is willing to sacrifice his life for them.

No, I don't think that's it.

At times I think marriage is a sacred institution that is indissoluble until death.

No, that's not it either.

At times I see Patricia as the only woman to whom I will be able to return when all the fiction that my life has become falls to pieces.

Maybe it's not even because of that. But today I wrote a letter to Carmen and I stuck it underneath her door. I don't remember the exact words. I don't even know if I began it with *Dear Carmen* or simply her name or if I went directly into explaining that I did not want to see her again. I guess that I did sign it at the end. It would have looked pretty bad if I had sent it anonymously. Yes, I definitely signed it, but was it as Froylán or as Juan?

As soon as I arrived back home, I cursed my habit of acting impulsively, and even though it was just another impulse, I went back to her apartment hoping to recover the letter. I devised a plan along the way. Maybe Carmen had not found it yet, so that by sticking a sheet of paper underneath the door, I could get back the envelope by pulling it back out. The plan's success hinged on the envelope's not being farther away than the distance within reach of a legal-size sheet of paper.

Once I was there, kneeling beneath the number 147-B, I wanted to see myself as a hero in a spy movie; however, I could only picture a boy undoing the evidence of his latest prank. I quickly stuck the paper underneath, since doing it slowly would mean pushing the envelope farther inside. Then I pulled it out like a fishhook that hadn't caught anything. I did it two or three more times, trying different areas, until it was snatched away from me from inside. I had still not assimilated what had happened when the paper came back with a message written in pencil: *At least be man enough to live with your decision.* The opened envelope appeared immediately. I picked it up like a deflated balloon, not knowing whether to knock on the door or to say anything.

I returned home defeated, tempted to show the letter to Patricia and complain to her, "Look what I did for you." She would be eternally grateful. "Thank you for choosing me over that woman." And then I would have the right to insult her and hit her every time I felt like making her pay for my disgrace. She would say to me, "Yes, I accept it, I deserve it."

But again, those were just impulsive ideas, just as it was an impulse to throw the letter down the toilet, pick up the phone, and call Carmen.

"It's me," I said.

"What do you want?"

"Did you read the letter?"

"Yes, and it made me laugh."

"Why?"

"One thing is to write fiction for an old man, and another thing is to write it for me."

"Then can I see you again?" I regretted the question. It was what Carmen expected: more evidence of my indecisiveness. I would regret my next question even more.

"The odds are against you," she said, smiling no doubt.

"By how much?"

"What do you mean 'by how much'?" she asked, bothered, I guess, because of my insistence in speaking by means of questions. "Do you want an amount or something like that?"

I nodded yes in order to get brave and then I said, "Yes."

"Give me a number from one to one hundred."

Seventeen had always been my special number, full of power. I had always thought that the union of the 1 with the 7 would make a great difference in my life.

"Seventeen," I said firmly.

"I would have preferred that you hadn't left me to chance," she said, and hung up.

From the living room I could see the shifting shadows created in the bedroom by the light from the television. Patricia and the nine-o'clock soap opera. I clenched my fist tightly and walked toward her. I looked at her for a while: she was just as immersed in the weeping of the protagonist as in the commercials for insecticide. I relaxed my hand. She lowered the volume and with a few pats on the pillow invited me to join her.

"Who were you talking to?"

"Nobody." I lay down next to her to watch the soap opera.

"THE SEÑORA SAYS NOT to come anymore."

"Why?" Juan was surprised. "Go and ask her."

A few minutes later: "She says because you are not Señor Doménico anymore but rather that fellow Juan Crapistrán."

"Capistrán."

"Yes."

"And what difference does my name make?" he asked as he was
thinking about how quickly the priest spread news. "Aren't I still
the same person?"

"Well, to me you are the same, but let me check with the
señora."

The door remained open, but an invisible barrier blocked his
way. The short step from the front stoop to the inside hallway was
an insurmountable wall, a boundary open to Doménico but closed
to Juan Capistrán.

"She says you changed the story because of money. That everything was just fine when you were Doménico because she could only fall in love with the man in the letter. And now since you have another name . . . well, it's not the same anymore."

"She told you that?"

"More or less, but her words were much angrier. She also told me some things that I didn't understand about an iguana's tongue."

"And there is no way to work this out?"

"Look, I think that if you are determined to—"

"The question is not for you."

"Ah, wait just a minute."

Lerdo Street was one of the steepest in the city, since it began down at the river, next to the washing place, and ended at the Cerro del Camposanto. Therefore, the women who carried the baskets of dirty clothing on their heads would take huge strides, stepping first with their heels; and those who brought the clean clothing sweated with every step, tired of so much scrubbing, the steep slope, and the damp clothing that weighs more.

"She says no."

"Now ask her if—"

"Concha!" Carmen's cry was heard from a corner of the house.

"Excuse me, I'm going to see what she wants."

The people who were passing by and saw Juan, insistent with the servant, patient in the face of what seemed like so many rejections, assumed he was a salesman or a debt collector.

"She says that I should close the door now."

"Tell her to go to hell," he wanted to say, but he just thanked the girl and said good-bye with a handshake in which he wanted to convey to her all his misfortune. A shiver ran through Concha's body because Juan struck her as an attractive man. He began to walk away.

"Señor Capistrán," Carmen said from the balcony.

"Yes?" He turned and looked up. It was five o'clock, and the June sun was still intense.

"If you see Doménico, please give him this."

A handful of yellowed little papers flew through the air, falling onto the ground like injured butterflies. Juan instinctively began to pick up the pieces until he imagined Carmen smiling from the balcony.

"To hell with it," he said, and left without looking back.

FOR THREE NIGHTS I kept an eye on the cemetery walls, walking through the adjacent streets like a guard: slowly, with my eyes wide open. Finally, I saw him beneath one of the streetlamps. First I made out the outline of a bicycle next to the wall and then the silhouette of someone who I thought must be him. He was painting with a thick brush. He did not take off running like any other graffiti artist would have done upon hearing me approach; on the contrary, he finished his sentence: *I am falling because I let you go.*

"Pinez!" I shouted at him.

He continued working; only the signature was missing. I went over to him and gave him a pat on the back with the familiarity of an old friend.

"She left you, too?" I asked him.

"Yes," he turned around, surprised, "but you say 'too' as if you were talking about the same woman."

"No, I suppose they are not the same."

Carefully, he put the lid back on the can of black paint and wrapped the brush in a piece of onion paper.

"Let's go have some beers."

"Thanks," he said, "but it's very late."

His refusal seemed more due to suspicion than to the time. And who wouldn't be suspicious of a ghost in the dawn who watches him, pats him on the back, and invites him to go out for a drink?

"Then lend me your paint so I can write something."

"You can have it," he said, offering me both the paint and the brush. "This was the last thing I will write."

I took them and watched as he got on his old bicycle, on which he would no doubt set out before dawn to deliver bread or newspapers. He disappeared into the darkness, long before the squeaking of the pedals died out.

I opened the can and, nervous that a cop might come and catch me, was not able to think of anything appropriate. I could only write: *Damn Carmen.*

THAT APRIL 17, LEANING AGAINST a huisache tree and stirring up the flowers, Juan Capistrán waited for Carmen for three hours. Several wagons, carriages, horses, and mules driven by old friends and new passed by. All waved a festive good-bye, pretending that this was a vacation from which they would return in a little while and which they would talk about and that from the end of Don Porfirio Street, the whistle of the locomotive and the hissing of the steam would be heard.

"See you soon, Juan."

"See you soon," he responded.

And the wagons, carriages, horses, mules, and the waving hands disappeared behind the first hill, along with the dust.

"See you later, Juan."

"See you later, Madariaga."

He saw Carmen coming; she was wearing a brown dress and

her hair was unkempt. She did not seem to be in a hurry like the others.

"Carmen!" he shouted when she was near.

She wanted to pretend not to notice, but the horse stopped when he heard the voice, and not even the lashes from the whip made him move.

"Yes, señor."

"It's me, Doménico."

"No, señor. I think your name is Juan."

"Look, Carmen," he said, showing her the chest, "these are your flowers."

The horse began to walk, but now it was she who stopped.

"Mine?"

"Yes, I saved one every Wednesday."

"Thank you, but you keep them," she said, softening her voice, as if she had suddenly recognized the Doménico from before.

"They can stay, but I am going with you."

Carmen's hands hesitated, not knowing whether to relax or hold their grip on the reins. She looked at the road that stretched out in front of her, a solitary, dusty road that would soon be in darkness.

"All right," she said with her hollow eyes in tears, "get in."

And the wagon, with its new passenger, disappeared behind the first hill.

THE VIEJO CAPISTRÁN PICKED up the two sheets of paper with his sweaty, trembling hands. Of all the pages I had written, he would have to make do with reading only the last two. He looked carefully at each word, as if decoding a hidden meaning. He read the text slowly, or maybe he read it several times, since it took him more than ten minutes. Finally, he put the papers down and leaned back in his chair, exhausted and tense. He breathed deeply until he was noticeably more relaxed.

"What is this, Froylán? A fairy tale?"

I did not know how to respond.

"Who are you trying to fool with such stupidity?" he went on, bothered.

"You told me—"

"Yes, you don't have to remind me, but you can't change things like this. You have Carmen; I never had her: that is something you must understand."

I wanted to tell him that I never had her either. I wanted to leave that place and never go back, leave him with his fairy tale, with his old folks, his one-eyed friends, and his nuns. I chose to save my writer's pride.

"All right," I said to him. "I'll come back tomorrow."

THE NEWS CAME SUDDENLY. The concession to build a railway from Tampico to San Luis had been awarded to a company called The Mexican Railroad. The route would pass through a string of unimportant towns: Ventura, Cerritos, San Bartolo, La Canoa, Tamasopo, Valles, Las Palmas, Tamuín, Perseverancia. And Tula? the people asked. There is no mention of Tula. It must be a mistake, surely it is a mistake or a joke, or a despicable lie. If we have always been the midway point between Tampico and San Luis, why does the route now go that way? Everyone agreed and clung to the possibility that it was a mistake, a joke, or a lie. Although looking at it carefully, Madariaga said, opening up a map on the table and moving his index finger along the potential route, the journey is shorter if it does not pass through Tula. They called him a traitor and a sellout, and his only response was that mathematics never fails, that the shortest distance between two cities will always be a straight line. In the capital, the authorities kept working on railway issues, and the other concessions were soon given out. Everything coming from the United States would now follow a route from Matamoros to Monterrey; and Monterrey, that same city that to communicate with the capital by telegraph had used our cables and our route, decided that it was one thing to send messages and another to transport cargo and passengers, and it laid down its rails far from us. The map of Mexico was filling up with lines like scars, lines that connected the north with the south, the Gulf with the Pacific; lines that meant realities and projects, that approached cities, seas, mines, countryside, businesses, and lovers; lines that marked the boundary of a large and isolated territory whose center was Tula—the only one of the large cities that was left without one of those lines. They want to distress us. Distress us? Isunza asked, they want to screw us. After ranting about everything for a while, the question arose: What to do? We are going to announce the Tula Plan, to rise up in arms, to overthrow the president, to return to the monarchy, to invite a foreign prince, to... And after many ideas, one came up that seemed to be the best: we are going to write to Doña Carmelita, since it must mean something to be a *Tulteca* and she must have married Don Porfirio for something. There was much applause and Maestro Fuentes said, I agree, but we need to be more diplomatic. First we name the two main streets after them and we write them a letter notifying them of this. Then we will have the right to ask for a favor. The next day, long before the signs were ready with the names of Don Porfirio and Doña Carmelita for each corner, the news appeared in *El Tulteco*. In a touching ceremony presided over by the highest authorities in our city, the streets that were previously called Hidalgo and Libertad were now renamed for our chief executive, hero of Puebla and Tuxtepec, and his distinguished wife and favorite daughter of Tula. The blessing was rendered by His Excellency... The announcement was cut out of the newspaper and sent to the Castillo de Chapultepec. It was immediately decided that a second letter would be sent two weeks later. This one would be full of drama and describe in detail the consequences of being left off the train route, reminding Carmelita constantly which land had been the first she had laid eyes on. Then came the waiting, the pouncing on the newly arrived mail sack from the capital, and the possibility, greater every day, that the letter to her or the one from her had gotten lost along the way.

AN UNUSUAL STIRRING WAS in the air from the earliest hours that April 17. A feeling of something dreadful, like a plague, like an enemy army on the other side of the hills, hung in the air. The only thing not moving was Juan Capistrán, who was leaning against a mesquite tree with a knapsack over his shoulder from which he would take out a taco whenever he was hungry. For him there was no rush, only impatience. He waited all day. He saw people go by, their faces blank, unrecognizable even though they greeted him with a good morning first and with a good afternoon later on.

The stream of people became thinner and thinner, and he thought that Carmen might have left via another road: the one to Tampico or to San Luis, but not this one, which went to Victoria, this one that was full of holes and dust, with a steep incline that would kill the mules before they had crossed the Sierra Madre, and which, because it was so narrow, would sometimes hurl distracted muleteers or sleepy coachmen over its edge.

He took the chest of flowers and threw it far away. He figured that they had tricked him, that Carmen would never go by this spot, that all the *Tultecos* had conspired so that he would stay in that spot while she, who was probably the first one to leave, headed south or east.

Restless, he began to pace back and forth, keeping within five yards of the mesquite tree, without a single idea of what to do. Then he saw her. Her carriage was approaching quickly. She was wearing a green dress and her hair was tied back with multicolored ribbons.

"Carmen!" he shouted when she was close enough.

She kept looking straight ahead as if she had not heard.

Juan reached into the knapsack and took out his bronze dagger. He ran after the carriage and after the woman. Even though she sensed the danger, she did not want to look back. She just urged the horse to go faster. Juan caught up to her, and with a quick, forceful movement, he angrily plunged the dagger into where he imagined there would be soft flesh, the same flesh he had wanted to caress, stroke, lick.

He did not feel like pulling the weapon out, and he let go of it right there, in that uncertain place where he had driven it. A peaceful feeling came over him, one that he had not felt since that distant feast day of San Antonio. The consequences did not matter anymore: the important thing had been having the guts to confront Carmen.

He watched the carriage move off, counting the slow turns of the wheels. One, two, three . . .

If not for Carmen letting out a slight moan, Juan would have thought that he had just ripped the cushion of the driver's seat.

If not for Carmen, after losing control of the horse, falling, motionless to the ground, Juan would never have known what became of her.

I stood in front of the old man with the satisfaction of finally seeing my work finished. He grabbed the pages out of my hand. Unlike the time before, he now read quickly. I noticed this in the darting of his eyes, alive and hopeful.

I don't know if he had already reached the end when he began to tear the pages in half, again and again, for as long as his strength allowed. He threw the pieces at me.

"Idiot," he said, "first you bring me a fairy tale, and now this shabby piece of work."

My first impulse was to pick up the pieces of paper; but then I remembered how stupid Juan Capistrán had looked as he picked up the pieces of that letter that Carmen had thrown at him. I left the home without saying a word and feeling like finding another Toñito so I could punch him.

TWO OR THREE MONTHS went by before the letter finally arrived. The Señora Romero Rubio de Díaz greets with the utmost pleasure the hardworking people and lovers of their country, the *Tultecos*. And she wishes to tell you that your determination to secure the railway route through your city is laudable. Congratulations. But at the same time she informs you that the mapping of those routes is something that lies outside of her authority, which in itself is little or none, since she only considers herself, like our martyr of Independence, a servant of the nation. Nevertheless, she investigated the reason for the apparent oversight or omission of Tula along the Tampico–San Luis line, and she was informed by engineer Sebastián Gálvez that the problem is merely orographic. Or, in other words, it is impossible to build a railway line that can cross the Sierra Madre and end up in Tula. The señora did not want to finish these lines without informing you beforehand that she is ever aware of where she was born, and as proof of her goodwill, to be of use she has sent you a gift. Finally, there was the signature of a certain Manríquez, who many believed to be ficitious, along with the entire letter. And the gift? those present asked. General Pisco, who had been chosen to read the letter because of his clear, strong voice, looked naively into the envelope, looking for a bill of exchange or at least a ticket from the national lottery. Screw her! someone shouted, and everyone chimed in. She didn't even tell us by her own hand. Isunza, out of mere principle because it bothered him that men who had been drinking and who smelled like the land took to insulting a woman from a good family, decided to distract them from the object of their censure. Señores, just one moment. The letter says clearly that our problem lies in being located next to the mountainside. Now I ask you: Who is responsible for this? The people came out into the street in a kind of hurried pilgrimage, picked up stones from the road, and walked two blocks to the small square where the statue dedicated to Friar Juan Bautista de Mollinedo stood. Idiot, the woman who threw the first stone called him. The stone-throwing broke out in such force that there were two head injuries as a result of bad aim. After a few minutes the monument to the founder was just a pedestal supporting a shapeless mass, full of nicks, and a still legible plaque that read: *Friar Juan Bautista de Mollinedo, born in Portugalete and deceased in Madrid, came to these lands of Nueva Vizcaya and one day in the year of our Lord 1617, brought Christianity to us and gave us our patron saint, San Antonio of Padua.* The racket stopped because word had spread that Doña Carmelita's gift had arrived. Everyone walked to the main square and there they saw two men lowering a box big enough to bury six bodies. Two volunteers began removing the nails from it, and one after another the nails fell to the ground with a moribund clinking. The cover was lifted off, revealing gears, screws, metal plates, and a large package wrapped up in newspaper printed in another language. They tore off the wrapping and discovered the moon face of a clock with twelve evenly spaced black marks. Fucked-up old lady, what kind of joke is this? The temptation to stone the clock as well began to fester. But Father Nicanor, who had always wanted a clock, embraced it with an emotion similar to affection and told them to take it to the church. It will look perfect in the tower, he said. The many attempts to assemble the device failed, at which point it was considered a riddle with no solution, a gag from the president's wife. Nevertheless, the determination of the father succeeded and quite randomly all the pieces fitted together and after a week the hands were telling the time in Tula. The *horero* directed a desperate curse at Doña Carmelita and from that point on sensed that the end was near. He continued to announce the hour, even though he was no longer paid for it, always trying to get a few minutes ahead of the clock in the bell tower, but the people called to him to be quiet. He took to begging for a few months. After that nobody knew what happened to him.

"LET'S SEE IF IT'S ALL RIGHT now," I said as I handed him my new version of events.

He folded the pages in half and stuck them under his pillow. He turned toward me and I sensed that he wanted to talk.

"What? Aren't you going to read them?"

"Not now," he said, smiling nervously. "I trust that this time you got it right."

"Well, then, I'll see you later." I raised my hand to wave good-bye and left his room. He followed me, telling me to wait, and that it was important for us to talk. I chose not to do so, and I took a path that had a lot of furniture and steps that were too high for his wheelchair. I turned around when I got to the door, and saw him laboring to push aside a table in his way.

Once I was in my car, driving through the two-o'clock traffic in the September sun, I felt that I should have waited for him to find out what he wanted to tell me, to have said good-bye in a more affectionate way, or, at least, to have hugged each other for having finished my novel, his biography.

Later on I laughed at myself for having been so sentimental.

THIS IS NOT THE END, most said or thought, and even without the support of the president's wife, they decided to continue their fight. Why do we need them to tell us where the railway will pass through if right here there are people with enough money to build a railway around the world? Then the landowners thought like landowners, the merchants like merchants, and the businessmen like businessmen, ignoring the possibility of thinking like *Tultecos* or Christians or benefactors or at least like men. No, they said, we would gladly do it, but it's not so easy. First we have to get the concession from the government to insure the tax benefits and see how the lands that it will pass through will be affected; then the profitability of the railway must be guaranteed with a steady stream of passengers, and especially goods; and add to all that the required evaluation by an expert of the total initial investment, construction time and so forth. The idea to collect funds by raising some trade tariffs was promoted. I think, Madariaga said, aware of the general enthusiasm, that we would collect more if we solicited donations. And so it was done, and Madariaga himself was put in charge of collecting the money. The first few days there were lines outside his office like those outside the tortilla shop. Some left money, others jewelry. Madariaga did not want to accept animals, and he told those who came with cows, mules, young goats, or hens to go sell them and bring him the money. He said the same thing to a woman who wanted to give him some stamps. Who am I going to sell them to? the woman asked. I was next on line, and I gave her twenty pesos for them. The construction of the station began with some improvised plans and volunteer labor. The building was ready in about eight months and two hundred meters of tracks were built in front: one hundred toward Tampico, one hundred toward San Luis. Why meters and not varas? Isunza asked, and Madariaga, staring at the ground, explained, you have to understand, Doctor, our days of glory are over. Since Governor Alejandro Prieto declined his invitation to the inaugural event, it fell to Father Nicanor to unveil the sign with big blue letters that said **TULA STATION**. There was clapping, singing, liquor, dancing, lights, speeches, laughter, and a literary contest won by the judge of the Court of First Instance, a resident of Potosí named Manuel José Othón, who in addition to reading the winning poem, delivered a highly applauded speech on the importance of connecting his land with ours by train. Once the party was over, Madariaga asked the crowd that had gathered for additional contributions so the work could continue. And what we already gave? That was spent on the building and the stretch of tracks. But we gave you a fortune, someone else complained. Madariaga was going to talk to them about bills, revenue, and expenses when a cry begun by a few señoras began to spread: Thief! Madariaga ran as fast as he could with his awkward body toward the church, pursued by the mob. They did not catch up to him, in part because he ran as he hadn't run since he was a boy, and in part because nobody wanted the responsibility of being the first to reach him. About to die from the incitement, he bolted the door and asked the father for asylum. Asylum? Churches have not given asylum for a long time. And as Madariaga had no more breath to talk, he expressed himself with his tearful eyes and his hands in a begging position. All right, *hijo,* stay here for a few days, but if the people find out that the right to asylum is not valid, I am not going to defend you. Your life depends on their ignorance. He was there for a couple of days. Then he must have slipped out at night when no one was watching, maybe helped by a friend, since his family did not want to stand up for him. No one dared to organize another collection nor was anyone willing to give his money, not one cent. That is why the railway was never more than two hundred meters long.

Motionless and menacing, the telephone on the table was silent: it had to ring soon.

Patricia turned off the television, and after a few minutes of silence in which I thought she must be brushing her hair, she came out of the bedroom. She asked me what I wanted for dinner, and I told her I didn't care. I heard the bubbling of oil, and then I knew that in reality my stomach did not share my indifference. "I hope it's not scrambled eggs."

"They said a hurricane passed through Cancún," she raised her voice to give me the news of the day, "and it left behind a lot of damage."

"Ah."

"It looks like it's heading for the United States. Those gringos up in Texas must be scared to death."

"As far as I'm concerned, I hope they get it good."

I didn't hear her reply, but I imagined it to be, "Don't be that way, they are people, too."

The telephone rang and Patricia forgot about what she had on the stove and ran to get it.

"Don't answer it," I yelled at her.

"Why not?" she asked me, worried, vacillating between obeying me or answering it. "It could be something im—"

I lost my patience and began to walk in circles and wave my arms around in the air.

"But you are not going to touch it, even if it rings all night. And you know something?" Patricia was looking at me in disbelief, with one hand that couldn't help going for the phone. "Do you know? This call *is* an important one. It is not your mama asking you to bring her coffee, nor is it your friend, the fat one, asking if you can get together on Thursday. No!" The ringing was becoming sharper and sharper, more nerve-racking. "Now the call is for me. It's one of the nuns: she wants to inform me that there is a body at the home, a body that stinks, and she needs someone to do her the favor of taking it away, putting it in a box, and lighting candles for it; someone to pray the rosary even though it is not Wednesday, to give up good money so it can be embalmed and dressed in its best clothes so it looks like a doll in a store window. Come on," I challenged her, "pick up the phone and you'll be throwing a dead man on your back."

The telephone stopped ringing. A burning odor was coming from the kitchen, an image of boiling oil on the stove and on the floor. Patricia was crying.

In a matter of seconds, just the time needed to dial six numbers, the telephone rang again: one, ten, one hundred times. All night long. And all night long Patricia cried "because I sense a disgrace," she told me, and hugged me with all her might. I did nothing but listen to those rings that sounded like cathedral bells. "Let them toll in his honor."

JUAN CAPISTRÁN MUST have gotten up at the same time as always and, like that time before, asked to be bathed with toilet water. He must have passed through the entire home greeting the old people and the nuns, El Tuerto and Sister Guadalupe in particular, with whom he took the time to remember the past and laugh a little, a laugh insufficient to break the seriousness of the moment.

"Do you remember when Carranza's men came?"

"No, Señor Capistrán, I am not that old."

"Okay, but you must remember the shoot-out with Escobar's men four blocks from here."

"Not that either."

"I do," El Tuerto would say. "One of their bullets left me this way."

And remembering made the three feel young again, and the

pleasure of the moment kept them there all afternoon, engaged in conversations that little by little became filled with bitterness, bringing them back to the reality of the home, of their sallow skin, because inevitably the sentences would begin with "if I had" or "if I could."

Then, I am sure, the *viejo* Capistrán went to his room.

He took the two sheets of paper and looked at them without making up his mind to read them. He went over to the window and looked out at that world forbidden to him; he looked at that horizon that ended at the house across the street, at the traffic light at the corner, at that coming and going of people who would never turn around to look at him so as not to face the possibility that one day they, too, would be locked up in that place. But now, even though it was just once, the old man did not want to be ignored.

"Cowards!" he shouted at the pedestrians, and they answered him with more shouts and gestures.

There he was, shouting and enjoying it because the people thought he was crazy, until it grew dark and he could no longer make out the expressions on the faces. He went over to the bed and, with a great effort, got himself into it to prove that he did not need the nuns.

He stretched out his arms and picked up the two sheets of paper again. He read them over and over until he memorized them, until he believed them, until he was exhausted.

Later, when Sister Guadalupe came to ask if he needed anything, she was surprised to see that he had already gone to bed. She went over to cover him with a sheet and noticed his sleep was too calm, too light; a calmness that she envied with all her heart.

THE TRAIN TO TAMPICO, full of politicians, journalists, and elegant women, arrived on April 17, never passing through Tula. The *Tultecos* came out into the streets early in the morning, as they did during the fiestas, only now there was no market in the town square or bottles of liquor or songs to the patron saint, to the plaster figure that they would no longer carry on its platform. The tortilla shop: closed. The bakery: closed. The windows, the post office, the pharmacy, Dr. Isunza's clinic, the casino, the telegraph office, schools, and mouths: all closed.

Disorganized, they hurried, packed in haste, as if the death of Tula had taken them by surprise, as if it had not been announced since the first tie of the railway was laid down, or since the map that avoided the Sierra Madre was drawn.

The bells tolled in mourning. It was time to leave, time for the three processions to move forward along the three roads. Some murmured a complaint to God, others mumbled Maestro Fuentes's hymn. The others, the majority, were quiet.

As they were drinking at the Lontananza, Abelardo had said to Juan, "Let's go to Tampico."

"Why, Godfather? So we can see that after the train nobody wants to repair something as useless as a wagon?"

They said good-bye over and over. They drank the last bottle of Gringo Amigo, and Abelardo told Juan that he had sent a letter to Buenaventura.

"So if she comes to look for you, she won't find anything."

"So stay and wait for her."

"No, Juan, I can't. But in the end I left a message for her at home."

At the table in front of them, Pisco was also getting drunk and insisting that he would not leave without first firing his cannon at the church clock. At the end of the evening, Maestro Fuentes came in, drunk like they probably all were, and he began to sing a tune with the words of the poem from the literary contest. "That will be my destiny," he said as he finished, "to keep subjecting music to the lesser arts."

"See you later, Juan," Abelardo tried to say good-bye again.

"Good-bye, Abelardo." They got up and went their separate ways. Left behind were Doña Esperanza, her husband, and her daughters, left in a town that now accommodated them, with houses that were transparently silent, full of whatever did not fit in the wagons. On that very day whatever was left behind became part of a distant past.

Tula was bleeding to death, and Juan climbed up to the top of one of the hills so he could watch it all. He saw Carmen on the road to Victoria, he saw the walnut tree, the huisache tree, the mesquite tree, her pink and white dress, her carriage that was becoming smaller and smaller, her hair that was swaying back and forth as if to say good-bye to all that remained behind her. He heard the old clanging of Father Nicanor's bells, the death moan of the wind beating against the bars of the doors, and the gentle flowing of the river. Doña Carmelita's clock brought to mind Pisco's unfulfilled promise, and it showed seven o'clock as the sun was setting, and nobody was left to light the old kerosene lamps or the new gas ones.

Juan emptied the flowers from the chest. "How many are there? One hundred? Two hundred?" He didn't care anymore. For him, all numbers had lost importance, whether they were to express a quantity of money, a date, or an age. He spit at the foot of Don Alejo's altar and walked toward the cave. The sound of the rattlesnakes became louder and louder, until he felt himself swallowed up by darkness, by the smell of brine, and of waste.

I circled Carmen's apartment until it grew dark, my sole purpose to be close to her. I got bored after a few laps around and I realized that if I really wanted to win her back, I would have to act more decisively. But that would come later. I got home and Patricia ran to me to hug and kiss me.

"What's wrong with you?" I took her by the shoulders and, slowly but firmly, pushed her away.

"There was just a warning that the hurricane has changed its course and is coming this way, and I didn't know what time you would return."

I didn't notice until then that the whistling of the wind was not normal. I looked out the window: the traffic was still heavy, even though the trees were bending in the wind, even though the sky was filling with clouds, gray clouds matching my state of mind.

"Stop exaggerating," I said. "The hurricane won't come this way."

She began to talk about how we needed to put tape on the windows, collect drinking water, and disconnect the electric appliances.

"Even your television?"

She did not want to respond, since I had not really asked her a question. She looked at me irritated, trying to think of a comeback, until she decided to lock herself in the bedroom.

I came into the study to write.

I am thinking about Carmen and about the *viejo* Capistrán, and I hear the rain begin to beat against the windows. When the hurricane passes, the water will have swept them both away. I will be alone, looking for her for the rest of my days, looking for her tomorrow out on the streets or later, much later, from the window of an old folks' home, hungry for her, heir to a past that one day I shall pass on to another writer who is just as naive as I, and whom I will tell that I am his grandfather.

Or I can stop writing and get the car keys without caring about the damn hurricane or about how Patricia will come out of the bedroom and run through the house shouting my name; without caring about the moment when she goes outside to be sure that I have left and sits on the ground to wait for me, confused and distressed in the midst of windows that are breaking because of the wind, crushed by the weight of time, by the many hours that will suddenly tell her, "Your husband is not coming back."

I can go to Carmen's apartment and knock on the door until she opens it or until I knock it down. Carmen, Carmen, I will repeat her name, and I will take her by the waist and wrench from her everything that I am not. I can tell her that in Tula we have an unfinished life, a big house across from the square, a dusty grand piano that surely needs tuning, railway tracks to which we have to add meters and more meters and